SLASH & BURN

MOSH SERIES BOOK 3

SUSANNA ROGERS

Bucher & Reid

This is a work of fiction. Names, characters, businesses,
places, events and incidents are either the products of the
author's imagination or used in a fictitious manner. Any
resemblance to actual persons, living or dead, or actual
events is purely coincidental.

Bucher & Reid

Cover by Amygdala Book Design
978-0-6484920-3-0

ALSO BY SUSANNA ROGERS

MOSH SERIES
Holler & Howl
Down & Dirty
Slash & Burn
Light & Shade
Ride & Crash
Ground & Pound

YOUNG ADULT
Infiltration (Book 1)
Regeneration (Book 2)
Validation (Book 3)

Parallax Error

CHAPTER ONE

Lachie

Another day, another hangover. A couple of aspirin had taken care of the headache but there was no miracle cure for the nausea and sluggishness. And that was the least of my problems.

At least they'd cranked up the air conditioning at the bar. I loved being back in Nevada. Hated the heat. And I'd always had a soft spot for The Swamp even if it was a dump. Sometimes I still couldn't believe Nick had bought the place.

I leaned back in my chair. "What's taking so long with the renovations?"

He looked up from the other side of the table. "Problems with the planning authority. Austin's handling it."

Austin. Our ex-bass player, also an architect. I gritted my teeth. Better I didn't say anything about that particular subject. It hadn't been long since he'd quit the band and I was still pissed about it.

"We did up the bathrooms already, Lachie," Nick said.

"Yeah, I noticed. It makes going to the john less of a

life and death experience."

Nick laughed, glanced down at his phone on the table. "Andrew's nearly here."

I scowled. "Don't know why you made me get up at the crack of dawn for this."

"It's noon, dude." He gave me a concerned look that was very unlike him. "Hey, we don't want to lose another band member."

Which made me think of someone else. The words sent a pang through my heart and I wasn't exactly a pang-in-the-heart kind of guy.

Nick was overreacting, though. They all were. They weren't going to lose me just because a stalker had been sending me Facebook messages. Called herself Angel. And referred to me as her darling. I was not her fucking darling and I had enough shit in my life already.

"This isn't going to work. You're wasting your time." The only reason I was here today was to put an end to this latest idea.

Nick stood. "They're here."

"They?"

He'd told me we were meeting Andrew Shields, head of Shields Security, for a friendly lunch. I knew what friendly meant. Didn't know he was bringing someone with him.

Andrew ushered a young woman ahead of him through the door and strode toward our table. So did she.

This woman was the opposite of Andrew, a big African American guy—and I mean linebacker-sized—with a huge gleaming smile against dark skin.

Whereas she was very much woman-sized and shaped. She'd pulled her light brown hair into a ponytail that showed off her pale skin and gray eyes. No smile. Only composure, loads of composure, practically overflowing with it. Something I should have more of. I made sure my tongue wasn't hanging out of my mouth.

Andrew motioned toward me. "I'd like you to meet Jess Hermann."

I shook her hand, stopped myself from grinning like an idiot, though it was a close thing. "Hi, I'm Lachie Tyler."

"I know. Pleased to meet you." Jess sat beside me, poised and unperturbed.

"Would you like some drinks to start?"

Tara, the bartender or bar manager or whatever she was, appeared out of nowhere the way she often seemed to. She was Austin's girlfriend, which didn't exactly put her in my good books, but I was getting over it.

"Sparkling mineral water would be lovely," Jess said.

Andrew nodded. "Same for me."

Nick agreed. He seemed to be turning over a new leaf or some such crap and had been for a while.

"I'll have the Frankston IPA, thanks," I said, because one beer wouldn't hurt and I refused to bow to the pressure of the non-drinkers.

"The best beer in town." Tara smiled, made me feel as if she was on my side, which was kind of weird.

She came back with the drinks and left menus with us while we went through the usual banter about the band and people we knew. Nick talked about his family because he was in love all over again and couldn't help himself. Jess didn't say much. Not much for her to say when she was with three guys who'd known each other for years.

A waitress came for our food orders. Nick and

Andrew ordered stuff that sounded too much like health food for my liking. I stuck with the burger and fries while Jess contemplated the menu, a cute frown forming in her brow.

"The burgers are the best in town," I said. "Flame-grilled on toasted Turkish buns."

She handed back the menu. "You talked me into it."

A girl with an appetite. Not too many of those around, or not in my world anyway.

After the waitress left, Nick finally came out with it. "You know why we're here?"

"Of course I do. And I haven't changed my mind. I don't want this sort of—" I searched for the right word — "intrusion in my life."

"It's for your own safety."

That got my back up. As if he hadn't done any crazy shit and had his share of wild women throwing themselves at him.

He added, "This is coming from the whole band, not just me."

"The whole band? That's only you and Cooper." Our drummer hadn't been able to make it today. "Not a lot of us left."

"And Brett. He was the one who organized this."

Our manager had already spoken to me about this. I might be outnumbered but I wasn't outmaneuvered.

The last couple of messages from the stalker had been increasingly threatening, stuff about how she'd hunt me down if god told her to. It had freaked me out, not that I'd let it show.

I just wanted it all to go away. Maybe the person would get bored, move on, and the problem would disappear. This wasn't a part of my life and couldn't be happening. I mean, it wasn't as if we were One Direction or I was Justin Bieber with thousands of screaming girl fans. We had plenty of followers but they weren't so frenzied and generally knew when to lay off.

"When we're all together we've got security for the band." I spread my arms. "That's fine when we're touring but I've been through this with you. You and Cooper don't have personal bodyguards and I don't want that either. I don't fancy having a team of guys trailing me and watching my every move. I just want to live my life and I've got enough on my plate at the moment."

Nick knew exactly what I was referring to. My dad had gone through bowel cancer years ago and now it had come back with a vengeance, more aggressive, more surprising than the first time, though you'd think we'd have been used to it. Some things you don't get used to.

It felt as if the world was shifting beneath my feet. Maybe that was why I'd taken the news about Austin leaving the band so badly. I swallowed back the pain that had nothing to do with Austin and everything to do with my father.

The conversation slowed as our meals arrived. I'd never felt less like a burger and fries in my life, even though my stomach was telling me I should eat.

The place was bustling, the tables all taken, a wall of noise around us. This wasn't The Swamp that I knew. I used to feel comfortable here.

"Lachie." Jess's voice snapped me back to attention. "I don't know what else you've got going on in your life and that's not really my concern."

I tried to sound casual. "Everyone's got problems."

"But personal security is our business and I think your friend has a point."

"That's what I've been trying to tell you, dude," Nick said. "It's why Jess is here."

Because she was some sort of security guard? Was that what he meant?

Maybe it should have sunk in earlier but I'd been too taken by the sight of her and my head was still foggy from last night's booze.

I turned to her. "So you work for Andrew?"

"That's right."

"You don't exactly look the part." Understatement of the year.

Andrew leaned forward. "That's why she's perfect for the job. She's smart, anticipates problems, and doesn't hesitate to call for help if she needs it. Above all, she blends in. No one is going to look at her and automatically think she's your bodyguard, and that gives her one up on them."

I glanced at Jess, tried not to stare too much. I couldn't imagine in what universe he thought this young woman might 'blend in' because, to me, she had a serenity and a presence that made her stand out.

I ate a few of the fries on my plate. Not so bad. Pretty damn good, in fact.

Andrew continued, "You don't want someone who'll intrude on your life or cramp your style? Not a problem. Jess is very good at staying in the background but she'll be there if and when you need her."

I raised my eyebrows. "Do you really think I'll need her?"

"What do *you* think?"

I hated it when people threw my own questions back at me, especially when I was doing such a good job of avoiding the answers myself.

I turned to Jess. "Do you mind if I ask how old you are?"

"Twenty-five."

Same as me. "And how long have you been doing—" I waved my hand —"this?"

"Several years, on and off, but I've been training a lot longer than that."

"Yeah, what do you do?"

"I'm a kickboxer. Started when I was fourteen and fell in love with it." The faraway smile on her face told me she wasn't kidding.

"So you can pack a punch? Have you ever had to use this against someone?"

"I've done my share of door work at pubs and clubs, and I've been in a couple of altercations when I absolutely couldn't help it, but that's the whole point. Whenever possible, you want to avoid things getting to that stage."

"I wouldn't mind seeing you in action." It simply didn't gel with me that this slender female in jeans and a white T-shirt could be some sort of fighting machine. "And guns? I presume you guys carry?"

"When necessary, yes, but my best weapon is my brain."

I whooped with laughter, then looked around to see no one else was laughing.

Jess gave me a look so scary it shut me up quick and made me think Andrew might be right about her.

Nick raised his eyebrows. "Haven't you noticed the way our security guys work when we're at a concert or making an appearance somewhere?"

I shrugged. "What?"

"They're the reason we don't run into any problems. Because they have a sense for what's coming, get in early, and stop bad shit from happening."

I hated it when Nick was a smart ass. Hated it when he was right too.

"So you've been talking to Andrew?" I raised my eyebrows. "You got this from him?"

"Actually," Andrew said, "he's been *listening* to me."

And I wasn't. I got the message.

Problem was, I didn't want to listen. It was easier to hide my head in the sand and pretend everything was fine.

Still, a part of me had a horrible feeling that this thing with the stalker was one of those issues that was going to get bigger before it went away. Much bigger. It'd been eating away at me for a while.

Nick leaned forward. "Look, we don't want you to end up like John Lennon. We want to avoid that at all costs."

I swallowed. "Hey, I'd rather be alive than be a legend."

"There, you've said it. We'd rather you stayed alive too, Lachie."

Alive...

My dad was teaching me the value of life every day, the importance of being with the people who mattered, and how you should make the most of every day. Instead, I was wasting my days being hungover and my nights being drunk.

I held a hand out. "I'll think about it. That's all I'm saying for now."

Nick started to say something but I told him we

should eat and finished off the rest of my burger. My stomach felt a lot better after it had something in it that wasn't liquid.

We continued with some polite conversation, which made me suspicious because Nick didn't do 'polite'.

He cleared his throat. "One more thing."

"What?"

"You need someone with you twenty-four-seven."

"Huh? But that'd mean someone moving in with me."

Surely he didn't mean Jess. He couldn't be serious. I'd never lived with someone and wasn't that sort of guy. For one thing, the opportunity had never come up because I'd been too young when I'd been dating my one long-term girlfriend, and now I specialized in the short-term. I didn't want someone who was a permanent fixture at my place.

Nick wasn't done yet. "You need someone with you all the time, dude. You drink a lot and then you don't always know what you're doing."

A hand on my chest. "*I* drink a lot? That's rich coming from you."

"You're so busy having a good time that you're not looking out for anything else. If something bad happened, you wouldn't even see it coming."

I scowled. "When did you get to be so mature and responsible?" I held a hand out. "Don't answer that."

"Andrew explained this stuff to me. They call this close protection. *Close.* You need someone to move in and keep an eye on you."

"Well, that could be tricky. It might really cramp my style."

Jess scraped her chair back. "Honestly, that's the last thing you should be worried about."

My jaw tight, I couldn't bring myself to look at her, couldn't imagine her moving in with me, not in the way they meant. Because they weren't talking about her jumping into bed with me. That was something I had no problem imagining. They were talking about her shifting into the spare room and overseeing my every movement, and that was just downright weird.

"Think about it, Lachie." Andrew leaned forward, smirking. "Hey, would you like me to move in with you instead, buddy?"

He and Nick laughed. Jess smiled wanly, going along with it.

That's when it hit me. They were serious.

CHAPTER TWO

Jess

"Excuse me." I stood, desperate for a short break.

I'd needed a breather as soon as I'd laid eyes on the guy. That's how damn good looking he was, and not just because of the long blond hair and green eyes. There was something about the laidback, rock star cool that had got to me. He was slightly scruffy too. In a good way. Like, if he had to wear a tie, he'd choke to death.

Andrew had already briefed me about Lachie's stalker and told me a bit about how The Merchants were looking for a new bass player. Also that Nick had bought the bar and a woman called Tara was the new manager. I liked to be well informed.

The only bit that hadn't sunk in until now was how reluctant Lachie Tyler was when it came to getting his own bodyguard. He didn't want me here, that much I could work out.

I swept my eyes across the room as I headed for the bar. A habit. I always made sure I knew what was going on around me, something I'd bet Lachie didn't bother with.

Nearly every table in the room was taken. These

people couldn't possibly have been here for the décor so they must've come for the food, which I had to admit was good.

Tara was smiling at me before I reached the bar. She had her own thing going with the rockabilly clothes and a purple streak in her black hair. It almost made me jealous because I had to stick with blend-in-the-background clothes when I was on the job.

"There's quite a crowd today," I said.

"Sure is." She nodded. "Can I get you a drink? I'll bring it over."

"No thanks, I'm just after the bathroom."

She pointed toward the other end of the bar where two girls were knocking back shooters. "That way and to the right."

I'd seen the sign earlier and didn't need directions. I just wanted a chat. You never knew what you could find out.

Perhaps she saw the tentative look on my face because she added, "Don't worry, the bathrooms have been done up. They're the best thing about the place." She laughed.

"What about the main bar? Will Nick be renovating?" The place was a mess, the floor scuffed, and the newspaper stuck to the ceiling too weird for words.

"Yep. And it's going to look fantastic. Come back after it's done and you won't recognize The Swamp. I mean that in the best way possible."

Nick seemed like a genuine sort of guy. He hadn't been able to stop smiling when he'd talked about his fiancée and little boy. Heartwarming to say the least.

I glanced back at the table and strode into the bathroom. The two girls I'd seen earlier were fixing their makeup. Skimpy tops, short skirts, lots of skin, lots of hair. Plenty of giggling too.

I could hear their conversation loud and clear while I was in the stall.

"I don't believe you're going to do it." Excitement in her voice.

"I am. That's Lachie Tyler. This is my big chance."

"What? So you're just going to go up to him?"

"We both are."

"And you're just going to ask him to autograph your boobs?"

"Only one of them!" More giggling. "With the permanent marker. Then it's straight to the tattoo parlor."

"Oh my God."

Followed by more enthusiastic sounds and exclamations.

They were leaving as I came out to wash my hands. I wasn't sure which was permanent marker girl but figured she was probably the one with tattoos on the back of her legs.

Something inside my stomach twisted. I didn't have a problem with tattoos and had a couple of small ones myself, but Lachie Tyler's autograph slashed across your chest fell into the category of things you were likely to regret.

Heading straight for Lachie, I overtook the two girls as they staggered to the bar to finish off their beers, probably for some Dutch courage.

I leaned close to him. "Don't look now but two girls are going to come up and one of them is going to ask you to autograph her bare skin. Don't do it. Make up some excuse."

He shot me a disbelieving look. "Why's that?"

Couldn't the guy just do as he was told for once? Talk about frustrating.

Suddenly the two girls were there, just as I was sitting down. One of them asked for a photo and he obliged, standing up and putting his head close to hers while she took a selfie of the two of them.

The girl beamed. "Thanks so much."

"Could I please have your autograph?" The other girl's eyes widened as she handed him a marker.

"Yeah, sure." Doubt in Lachie's voice. "I don't have any paper."

She pulled the neckline of her T-shirt away, revealing way too much cleavage. "Sign right here."

"I, um… "

"Go on. I don't mind. I'd really like it."

He handed back the marker.

Her face dropped. "But… "

She settled for a photo instead and the two girls left. Relief washed over me and I wasn't even sure why. Maybe because I'd been young and stupid once too.

Lachie sat down and turned to me. "What was all that about?"

"She was going to get your autograph tattooed on her boob."

He grimaced. "Tattooed?"

I nodded. "As in forever."

"That happened to me once." Nick's upper lip curled in distaste. "Only it was a guy and it was on his arm. I had no idea."

"I'm kind of grossed out." The look on Lachie's face told me he wasn't exaggerating. "I don't want my name stuck on someone's tits for the rest of my life."

"Or *her* life," I added.

He held my gaze. "So you're not even my bodyguard and you're protecting me?"

"You weren't the one I was protecting."

I was completely serious. Nick whooped with laughter anyway.

My gut told me to get out of there and cut my losses because, above all, I knew where I didn't belong. I needed the job, needed to prove to myself I could do it, and then maybe, just maybe, I could make this work for me. But not if Lachie wasn't willing.

I stood. "Thank you for the lunch. Andrew will let me know if you decide to go ahead with anything."

Lachie got up too. "I'll walk you to your car."

I raised my eyebrows. "You'll walk me to my car?"

"You'll beat off any big, scary dudes, won't you, Lachie?" Nick laughed. Andrew too.

"You're such a douche," Lachie said over his shoulder as we left.

Despite everything, he made me smile as we stepped through the door. "How very gentlemanly of you to offer to escort me."

"I have an ulterior motive."

"And what's that?"

"I can't make you out. You mentioned you'd worked at pubs and clubs. Why?"

"A nice girl like me, you mean?"

"Yep. Arguing with drunk idiots and breaking up fights, that's got to be shitty work. What do you get out of it?"

I upped my stride. "It was a start into the security

business and I had the right skills for it. And, for the record, it wasn't always shitty. Most people were nice and there weren't that many drunk idiots."

Truth was, I got off on it. Nothing wrong with a bit of a power kick and I never misused it. Every interaction was another small piece of proof that I wasn't a scared little girl anymore. Or maybe I'd always been more sturdy than I thought.

"And you liked that?"

"Yep." I stopped by my car. "Sorry to disappoint you but we're here already."

He stayed, didn't look like he was going anywhere in a hurry. "So how did you get into this, *really*?"

I wasn't going to tell him my deepest, darkest secrets, not when I'd only just met the guy. I could give him food for thought, though.

"Would it surprise you to know I was a kindergarten teacher?"

He laughed. "What? From teacher to bodyguard?"

My contract had run out at the end of the previous school year and the principal's niece got my old position despite the fact I was doing an excellent job and the kids loved me. The unfairness of it still hurt, but I was moving on. I had to. I was grateful to Andrew and lucky, after all, to have the chance to make my night job into a full-time position.

"I was still working as a kindergarten teacher when I did my bodyguard training one summer," I said. "Andrew had already taken me under his wing by then and insisted I do it. He told me I'd love it and he was right. I was like a pig in poo."

Somehow it had never seemed so strange to be a

kindergarten teacher by day and security guard by night. Being a bodyguard was a natural progression from that.

I didn't want the kids I taught to go through what I had. I wanted to guide them in their growth, help them with their skills, and protect them. Protecting. It was what I did.

Lachie pushed the blond hair back from his face. "Aren't you worried about the risk? About getting into a dangerous situation?"

I shook my head, frustration simmering inside me. "It's all about avoiding those bad situations. Weren't you listening back there?"

"Sure I was."

It seemed to me that Lachie's outstanding personality trait was stubbornness. Along with those devastating green eyes which weren't exactly a part of his personality but were hard to ignore.

"Don't you get it?" I said. "Life is fragile. And one person could change your life, take away your freedom, leave you scarred."

His eyes narrowed. "I know exactly how delicate life is."

"You mean … your father?"

He nodded. I should have known. I was comfortable in the world of self-defense and personal protection. Not so much when it came to things like this.

"I heard about your dad," I said. "I'm sorry he's so unwell."

"What did Nick and Andrew tell you?"

"Not a lot. They don't gossip, Lachie, and they'd help you if they could." I held a hand out. "Sorry, I've said the wrong thing again."

His jaw tight, pain glimmered in his eyes. "No, I'm sorry. It gets to me sometimes."

Maybe he wasn't a shallow rock star who was used to having people pander to him after all. Maybe there was more to Lachie Tyler than met the eye. Because he had a father he cared about, someone he loved who loved him right back. And that gave him one up on me. Made my chest tighten.

"I think it's great you can be there for your dad," I said. "I'm sure he appreciates it."

Lachie swallowed. "He does."

"But if you're going to take care of him, you have to look after yourself first. He needs you safe and in one piece."

"I'm doing okay."

"I've seen the Facebook messages from your stalker, Lachie. That stuff about how you can run but you can't hide. How she's coming for you. Even her Facebook name is threatening. Angel Vengador."

The supposed surname meant 'avenger' in Spanish.

"They're just words," he said. "She hasn't actually done anything."

Despite everything, I felt for this guy who loved his father and was in denial about his stalker. He didn't deserve these things but, then, we didn't always get what we deserved. My throat tight, I gave myself a couple of seconds.

"Lachie, you can't handle this yourself. You won't know you're in danger until it's too late."

"I can look after myself better than you think. I grew up here in Frankston, remember? My life wasn't always fancy hotels and bottles of *Dom Perignon*. I don't even like the stuff. I'm more a 'beer' sort of guy. And I like my life the way it is."

"Then you should do everything in your power to keep it like that."

"I don't see why this is turning into such a big deal."

"But that's exactly it."

I bit back the words because I'd already told him we wanted to stop this person sooner rather than later.

At least I knew that if I got the job, I didn't have to worry about getting into a personal relationship with this guy. That'd put us both in a dangerous position because if I was distracted or too involved, my guard would be down and I wouldn't see trouble when it came my way. Luckily, I didn't go for guys who were anywhere near as stubborn as Lachie Tyler.

I dug a card out of my purse and passed it to him. "You've got Andrew's number and now you've got mine. I also train and teach at MacMillan Martial Arts if you want to come along. I'm there most nights."

"You think I'd be interested?"

"Well, you said you wanted to see me in action, or maybe you've forgotten already." I held back the resentment that'd been building. "Look, you can stay at home with a beer in one hand and a babe hanging off the other. Doesn't worry me. Or you can see what happens when you learn some discipline."

He smiled, wasn't offended. "You think I need more discipline?"

"I don't know. You've been very successful with the band. I'm sure that didn't happen overnight or by accident."

"You got that right. There was a lot of hard work

involved."

I stared at Lachie thinking that's what he was. A lot of hard work. And maybe he needed to be spurred into action. As far as I could tell, he hadn't considered that this job might be an imposition on me too because I had my own life and my own home, an apartment I shared with a friend.

I walked around to the driver's side of the car. "You don't need someone to hold your hand. You need someone to kick your butt."

And I knew just the person.

CHAPTER THREE

Lachie

MacMillan Martial Arts. The sign was lit by fluorescent lights. Kickboxing, mixed martial arts, Brazilian ju jitsu. I'd watched enough UFC to have some idea what was involved.

I pushed open the door. It wouldn't hurt to see what was going on in here, not that I found Jess Hermann intriguing. No, I was just very nosy.

A strange scent hit my nose as I trudged up the stairs. Strange and familiar at the same time. It was the smell of the boys' locker room, fresh sweat lingering with stale bacteria that was hanging in the air.

It reminded me of the exhaustion after a game, after we'd run our hardest and tried our best, after the endorphins had faded. A good sort of exhaustion. Rewarding.

I'd never been a jock at school but had played a bit of everything: basketball, baseball, football, and soccer. All team sports because I was a team player. Still was. That's what the band was—a team—even if not everyone acknowledged that.

It had been a while since I'd done anything resembling a sport. My enthusiasm had started waning some time during junior year at about the same time my interest in girls and booze started taking off.

At least I'd made it to the top of the stairs without panting. The dojo was pretty much what I expected, a big room with blue training mats on the floor, two walls lined with punching bags, and a boxing ring set up in a corner. A lot of sweaty bodies were packed into one place.

I'd figured it wouldn't hurt to see Jess in action at the martial arts place so I hung near the back, leaning against an unattended counter, my eyes set firmly on the most striking woman in the room who was, as it happened, striking.

Bam, smash, she hit the pads, then shoved her opponent back, and slammed in a kick. Impressive.

Seconds later, a young guy came up to me. "Can I help you?"

"I'm fine," I said. "I'm a friend of Jess. Just here to watch."

"Okay, I'll leave you to it."

He put his hands together and bowed his head, then got back onto the mat. He'd bowed. Wow. I didn't normally engender that much respect.

Jess spotted me, nodding in acknowledgement, then got on with teaching the class.

Something had come up since I'd last seen her, something that put my nerves on edge, my reason for being here. I bit back the anxiety.

She took control of the room and demonstrated the next drill for the class. The guy holding the pads was easily twice her size, concentrating hard, being pushed back against the power of her strikes. She'd said she could punch and kick hard, and now I believed her.

On one hand, this seemed like the same Jess I'd met at The Swamp. On the other, it didn't look anything like her. She was pumped, tight little muscles outlined beneath her glowing skin. As if she was possessed. As if something else had taken over her body.

"Then I want you to finish them off." She reached for the back of one pad. "Pretend you're grabbing them around the back of the head and lay in three big elbows." She demonstrated the strikes. "Just smash it."

I swallowed. I was right yesterday when I'd thought she looked scary. In the best way possible.

Then the class started doing the drill and she wandered around and offered some help to two guys. Smiling, she seemed to be back to the Jess I'd met before. After she finished with them, the two guys bowed as she was moving away. More of that respect I'd seen earlier.

The music industry could have benefited from a little of that. I knew The Merchants had it good now, but that was only because of some of the shit the so-called industry professionals had tried to sling at us earlier. Record companies, promoters, they were all the same, and now those exact people would suck up to us because we'd made it and they could make even more money out of us.

I gritted my teeth. I was doing the right thing. Truth was, I'd made my decision before I got here and seeing Jess in action was just an added bonus. A very nice bonus.

"Time, guys!" she yelled. "Swap the gear over. It's the other person's turn. Get started as soon as you're ready."

Jess strode toward me like a woman who owned the room. Because she did. Her T-shirt was drenched in sweat, stretched over boobs in what must have been one hell of a bra, and clinging to her abdominals. This woman was ripped. Also in the best way possible.

She looked at me with those clear gray eyes. "Lachie, I wasn't expecting you."

"Should I have called?"

"It's what people usually do, but I don't mind. Did you want to have a look around or was there something specific you were after?"

"I'll pass on the ass kicking." I smiled. "Though I have no doubt you could do exactly that."

"It's fun. I love this stuff. Like a pig in poo, remember?"

"So I'm safe walking down the street with you?" I laughed.

"I don't know about that. Maybe you're not safe at all. Maybe that's why you're here."

She'd nailed it. My stomach sank. "Can we talk?"

"Absolutely. Do you want to take a seat? I'm nearly done here."

I sat on a chair by the wall while she resumed teaching. After the class was over, the young guy who'd come up to me when I first walked in came up and shook my hand, his eyes wide, his handshake enthusiastic. He had a few friends with him.

"You're Lachie Tyler." He slapped a hand to his forehead. "I can't believe I didn't recognize you. Then the other guys told me."

"Yep, that's me."

"Could I get a photo?"

"Sure."

He took a selfie with the two of us, then thanked me

profusely. Four girls were next, all of them eager for a picture so we decided on a group shot.

The room started emptying, except for some serious looking guys who were hanging around the boxing ring, putting on their gloves, deep in discussion. Fight strategies perhaps. Or maybe just talking trash.

Jess came back. She'd changed into shorts that showed off her lean legs and a clean T-shirt with a windbreaker thrown over the top, not that this did anything to hide those boobs or abs. That was one hell of a figure.

She took a seat beside me and pointed at the guys at the far end of the room. "I usually stay for the sparring session."

"Not tonight?"

"No, I figured you came here for a reason."

Now I was getting in the way of her training, something I hadn't considered. I'd thought it the other way around, that she'd be impinging on my lifestyle.

Nerves settled in my stomach. I knew why I was here and at the same time, I didn't want to admit it. I was supposed to be a man, strong and invincible, the one who took care of others, not someone who had to call out for help. It had been eating away at me since the delivery late this afternoon.

I looked down at my hands. "Fans send gifts all the time. Sometimes they go overboard and send panties and bras, so after a while you kind of get used to things being a little weird."

"Go on."

"The stuff would usually be delivered to hotels when we were touring. Often it can be pretty easy for people to work out where we're staying."

She nodded, gave me the space I needed.

"My stalker sent me cookies." I realized how dumb this sounded, how lame.

Jess leaned forward, raised her eyebrows. "Cookies?"

"Cut into the shape of guns."

That got her attention. "Where'd she send them?"

"To my home."

She knew where I lived. My stalker had said as much before and now this proved it.

My home, the one place I could be myself, where I wasn't famous and didn't have people chasing after me, where I was just a guy who played guitar. My gut twisted.

Jess nodded and took a moment. "You sure the cookies were from her?"

"There was a card. *From your angel.*"

"It's strange. The idea of cookies is almost motherly, as if she wants to take care of you. But guns, no, there's nothing friendly about that. And she's never sent anything to your home before?"

"No one has."

"Have you been to the police?"

"To tell them someone gave me cookies?" I shook my head. "I was going to call Andrew but I came here first."

It had taken me long enough to gather the courage, despite the fact I'd known Jess would be the right person to take care of this. I didn't want to concede weakness. Didn't want to admit someone else into my life either.

"How was the parcel delivered?" she asked.

"Through the regular postal service."

"What's your home security like?"

"What security? The usual, I've got an alarm, locks on the doors and windows."

She slid her hand onto my knee, the warmth of her touch comforting. Comforting and … something else. This was the first time she'd touched me and if I had anything to do with it, it wouldn't be the last.

"I'll follow you in my car and come home with you," she said. "I'll call Andrew so he can meet us there. We'll do a sweep of the house. Better to be on the safe side."

I liked the way she took control. It took me by surprise. I hadn't known it would be like this.

"Sounds good," I said. "So you'll stay?"

"I'll stay."

Before, I hadn't wanted anything that would cramp my style. I wasn't so sure now. Maybe Jess Hermann wouldn't be such a terrible intrusion into my life after all.

CHAPTER FOUR

Jess

Andrew and I had taken a good look around Lachie's house the other night. Though not huge, the place had one of everything, one pool, one hot tub, one music room, one spare bedroom. More than one actually.

I'd had a couple of days to settle in, but I was never going to feel completely relaxed here, and that was as it should be. Even though it might not look like it, I was working and had to be attentive, fully present in body and mind.

Nick had come by and I'd met Cooper, the drummer. Lachie and I had been to visit his parents, to the store, for drinks with a friend, all normal interactions, and all uneventful. Just the way I liked it.

We'd been to the police station, and they'd documented the event and taken the cookies and container for testing and fingerprinting. The stalker had fingerprints—no surprises there—but they didn't correspond with anyone on record and there wasn't much else the police could do for the time being.

Lachie was on the phone on the back patio, elbows

resting on his knees, long blond hair hanging over his face. He'd gone out there for some privacy so I left him to it, but kept an eye on him through the glass doors from the living room.

It wasn't hard to tell something was wrong, no matter how much he tried to cover his face and his feelings. His dad had bowel cancer and I gathered his treatment wasn't going so well.

Outside, Lachie pressed his eyes shut, the phone still to his ear. Pain was etched in the frown between his eyes and the brackets that appeared around his mouth when he got stressed. The whole family was struggling with this.

He took the phone from his ear, turned it off, held it in his hand, and stared at the paving, the same pained expression on his face. Concern simmering in my stomach, I wanted to reach out to him but every time I did, he either ignored me or played it down.

I couldn't blame him. I wasn't a friend. I was the hired help, not right for this particular job.

Eventually he got up and stumbled inside the house, closing the door behind him.

I stood up. "Everything okay?"

A pathetic question under the circumstances but it was the best I could do. Lachie didn't look at me, not so much as a glance, and didn't lock the door either. He trudged out of the room without a word.

I took a deep breath, swallowed back the resentment, told myself this was his house and he could do as he wished. He was in pain—I could see that—not that it made me feel any better. I locked the rear door and sat back down.

Minutes later, the first chords from his guitar rang

through the air, angry at first, then calmer. The music room wasn't soundproof and maybe that didn't matter when you lived alone. He shifted from one song to a different one, from one riff to another, with such ease and fluidity that you could hear how natural this was to him. Almost like speaking.

Then a lot like yelling and screaming. Because when it was loud, the guitar would roar, blasting through the walls, filling every room with its power. It could be beautiful—and scary—resonating through my entire body.

An hour passed. Then he'd play part of a song, followed by silence, and he'd play again.

I waited till the music petered out, then strolled across and knocked on the door. Lachie pulled it open and nodded for me to come in, looking very much like a changed man. I let out a sigh of relief. For me. For him too.

He tugged the lead out of the guitar and grinned as he strummed the strings. "Much quieter now it's not going through the amp."

Wandering inside, I took in the guitars hanging on the wall, lots of them, another on a stand beside him, a couple of big black amplifiers, and a pile of books on the carpet in the corner. Books, I wouldn't have picked it.

"I'm lucky," I said. "I got a free concert."

"I'm glad you think that makes you lucky." He smiled. "Have a seat."

I dropped down onto an office chair that looked more comfortable than the stools. Lachie flicked off some switches on the amplifier in an easy movement that told me he'd done this hundreds of times before.

"It's not so surprising," I said. "I like the band. I like

your guitar playing."

He raised his eyebrows. "You sure it wasn't too loud for you?"

"Oh, yeah, it was. Way too loud and I loved it. I like the way it goes loud, quiet, loud. The quiet bits make the loud parts seem louder. It gives it more power, more emotion, more drive."

He tilted his head. "Have you ever played in a band?"

I laughed. "Me? I can't play an instrument to save my life but I know what I like. Your playing reminded me of some old Nirvana songs, not that you were copying, but in the feel of it."

"That's high praise." He leaned against the amp, grinning. "So you like the old stuff. What about The Pixies? That's where Nirvana got it from. Or so they say."

"I've never heard of them. I mean, I've heard the name but I don't know the music."

"They're a brilliant band. Very influential. Like The Velvet Underground."

Another band I'd barely heard of. I didn't say anything and nodded for Lachie to continue.

"There's the old saying that The Velvet Underground didn't sell many records but everyone who bought one went out and started a band. Pixies are a bit like that."

"Hmmm."

He shrugged. "I can't help being a music nerd. It's part and parcel of being a musician."

My eyes narrowed. "You know a lot about this stuff but I bet I could beat you in a quiz about Bruce Lee, boxing, and UFC." I brought my fists to my face and shadowed a couple of quick punches.

"I bet you could too."

I liked the smile on his face now that he was back to his old self.

"You look at home with your guitar."

He lifted the strap over his head and placed the instrument on a spare stand. "I don't know how Nick does it."

"Does what?"

"Stands on stage without his guitar. He does that for a few songs. Man, I'd feel like I was standing there with my dick hanging out."

I laughed, clapped a hand to my mouth.

He sat down on one of the stools. "Too much information?"

Way too much. I didn't answer. If I pictured Lachie in any way, shape, or form, it had to be with his pants firmly on. Besides, he looked good in a pair of jeans. Slim hips, tight butt, there was a lot to like.

"So, are you going out later?" I asked.

"You mean *we*. Are *we* going out?" A muscle flinched in his jaw, his lips thin. "There's no 'me' anymore." He held a hand out, composing himself. "I'm sorry. I shouldn't take this out on you."

I gave him a few moments, then asked, "Do you want to talk about it?"

He got up, picked an acoustic guitar off the wall, sat down, and started strumming softly.

After a while, he said, "Dad's cancer doesn't seem to be going away." His voice cracked. "So whenever I call, whenever I see them, it's never good news. Mom said I shouldn't come around today, not to bother him, that Dad was dozing all day."

"Maybe he needs to rest."

A curt shake of his head. "You don't know my family. That was code for 'Dad is doing really crappy and can't bear for you to see how sick he is'. As if I can't work it out."

"I'm sorry."

"He's a great guy, my dad. He doesn't deserve this."

A pang shot through my heart at the pain in Lachie's eyes. I'd bet the pang in his heart was a hell of a lot bigger.

"My mom's wonderful too," he added. "She does an amazing job looking after him and most of the time, she manages to look after the rest of us too. I guess moms are like that."

Not mine. I didn't say anything. I felt lucky, though, to have my aunt and uncle, and had no clue what I'd have done without them.

Eventually, I asked, "Do you have any siblings?"

"An older sister, Claire. She got married last year and is hanging out to have kids but her husband wants to wait a couple of years. God knows my parents would love grandchildren." A pause. "If my dad lives long enough to see them."

"Is it really that bad?"

His lower lip trembled. "It shouldn't be this way. I've done everything I can, bought the best care for him, but the best doesn't seem to be good enough."

So he was paying for his dad's treatment. "Does that mean your parents couldn't afford this on their own?"

"They would've struggled. I didn't want them to worry about it. I wanted them to proceed with the doctors' recommendations without having to think about the repercussions for their bank account. Because they should be concentrating on Dad's health and getting better."

"That was good of you."

"For what it's worth. I've got all this money and it's not helping, not enough. My dad's life is still hanging in the balance. I still can't make sense of it." His eyes narrowing, he became louder, more worked up. "You can have all the money in the world and it doesn't mean jack shit. It wasn't like this before. Money was buying me a hell of a lot of happiness. I thought I had it all. Now this."

There was no easy fix. He'd worked that out.

"You're helping though," I said. "You must be making a difference."

He looked down at his hands. "Growing up, Mom and Dad were the best. Didn't matter that we weren't exactly loaded. Dad was always throwing a ball to me, helping me with sports, and tried to help me with my homework too but I wasn't so interested in that. He showed me how to fix my bike and do loads of other stuff too."

He made them sound like some wholesome TV sitcom family, which wasn't quite the picture I had of them. I'd seen their pain. It was hard to see much else.

"That's nice," I said weakly.

"Sorry?"

"I just mean it's good that you appreciate your time together and your upbringing."

He waited, looked across at me. "What about you?"

The question took my breath away, only for a moment. My parents called themselves free spirits but that only meant they didn't want to be bothered with me.

Not that I minded being an accident. And my parents loved me. In their own way. But it was always so blatantly clear to me that I constantly got in the way of what they wanted. And that made me *feel* unloved.

I swallowed back the hurt. "My parents aren't like your normal, everyday family. They're like hippies, only without the long hair and beads."

"A lot of good music came out of those times." Lachie's voice softened. "The Byrds, The Doors, Hendrix."

So now he was changing the topic when he was the one who'd asked in the first place? It rankled.

"My folks aren't musicians," I said. "They just want to do their own thing. They didn't think they should have jobs like regular people. A few years back, they moved to a settlement in California where they live simple lives growing their own vegetables and smoking lots of grass."

He smiled. "Your parents smoke weed? Isn't it supposed to be the other way around?"

"Everything was the wrong way around with my mom and dad. I used to put my alarm on in the morning to get them out of bed and then point out to Mom that I had school and homework." All of which had made me very self-sufficient because I had to work everything out myself. "And as a teenager, I couldn't stand the smell of pot. Still can't."

The look on Lachie's face told me he didn't quite get it, and sometimes neither did I because I still couldn't understand how my parents could think it was okay to go off and leave me at age sixteen with Aunt Rachel and Uncle Mark. I'd been more grown up than other kids my age, but not *that* grown up. I wasn't made of steel.

Surely the incident on the bus had told them that. I'd only been a kid and had fallen into a heap, but they managed to forget so much. I bit back the resentment.

I hadn't come to the music room to inquire about

Lachie's personal wellbeing even if that was the way it had turned out. It was his physical safety that was my priority and I couldn't forget it.

I stood. "You left the back door unlocked when you came in from outside."

"Yeah?"

"You need to make sure you lock it every time. When you're in here playing guitar, anyone could come in and ransack the place and you wouldn't hear a thing."

"That's why I've got you." He didn't bother hiding the displeasure from his face and voice.

"It's not hard to lock the door. Pretty simple, really, and you've got to get into the habit. I'd also like you to think about installing surveillance cameras around the property. It's not expensive for a guy like you."

"Maybe a guy like me doesn't want them."

Frustration bubbled inside me. Petulant, recalcitrant, there were plenty of words I use to describe him.

"Cameras only capture what's happened after someone's got in," he added.

Which was true. "And they can also help identify intruders."

I left while I was ahead. The way he had his head in the sand rankled. I almost wished I hadn't brought the subject up, except I had to. That was what I was here for.

Still, I'd liked the Lachie I'd seen before that so much more and maybe, just maybe, I could see where he was coming from and a kindness in his heart he was reluctant to admit.

CHAPTER FIVE

Lachie

Mom told me Dad was sleeping. Again. I didn't believe her. Then came the rumble of a deep voice from the other end of the phone. Dad's voice.

"He's awake, Mom," I said. "I can hear him."

Holding back the ache in my voice, I glanced up at the guitars hanging on the wall, a Gibson 335 and a Firebird. This was the one room of the house in which I'd always felt most comfortable. I could come to the music room and be myself, because who was I if I wasn't a musician?

I wasn't getting that snug-as-a-bug feeling right now, as my mom used to say when I was a kid. Instead, my chest felt tight, my breathing strained so much that sometimes it felt as if I couldn't breathe. All because of my dad.

"I don't mind you phoning, honey." Mom was using her calm-and-controlled voice. "You can call whenever you like, but we've talked about this. You don't need to worry so much. You should be living your own life."

"I am. And I'd like to speak to Dad please."

Damn it, I loved her so much it hurt. Loved Dad too.

Surely it wasn't meant to be this way. Love wasn't meant to equal pain.

The two of them were trying to put on brave faces but it wasn't hard to work out that the more Mom smiled, the more she was hurting underneath.

And Dad tried to hide all the time—from me and my sister, from his cancer, from the truth. The chemotherapy hadn't worked and now the doctors said they'd have a better idea of his condition after surgery, but Dad had fought against that too. Said he'd rather take his chances than get a colostomy bag. We'd talked him through that one.

"Your father is every bit as stubborn as you are," Mom said. "And he insisted he needs to spend the day dozing in bed. On his own."

"Okay, I won't bug you again today, Mom. But I'm not staying away forever and I'm not putting up with this."

"Honey, you're not bothering me. That's not it at all."

"No problem. I'll be around soon, just not today. Maybe tomorrow. Love you, Mom. Give Dad a big hug from me."

I hung up before she could argue because I planned on being there tomorrow.

Taking a deep breath, I put my phone down on top of one of the amps. A distraction, that was exactly what I needed.

I picked up my Les Paul and sat back down again. I'd always been a Gibson guy and, for me, this old guitar was the ultimate. A genuine 1960, not a reissue, it was the perfect color, cherry sunburst that had faded so it was amber colored on top. Man, I loved this guitar.

For years, it had been my dream to own something as

beautiful as this. Now all I dreamed about was my dad getting better. Sometimes I couldn't get rid of the ache inside. Couldn't bring myself to plug the guitar in either, not yet.

I drummed my fingers on the arched top. Dad's health wasn't my only problem. My stalker had sent another message. *Your angel is closer than you think.*

Not that fucking close. My blood started boiling right away. I didn't even know who that stupid bitch was, but there were times I just wanted her to come and get me so I could get the whole damn thing over with.

I was sick of her, sick of everything. I needed a night to remember how things should be, time to be myself, an evening where I could forget all the shit in my life.

And I knew exactly how to go about it.

The Les Paul went straight back onto the stand as I picked up my phone, my heart racing at the thought. This was long overdue. This was what I did, a part of who I was, and if anyone deserved to let out some steam, it was me.

Party at my house tonight.

I kept the messages short, one after the other, because my friends could work it out and if they couldn't, that was their tough luck. Already, the effect of deciding to have a party was like a muscle relaxant and I could almost feel the party vibe and taste the alcohol.

Booze, that reminded me. Where was the number? I scrolled through my phone till I found Bar and Beyond and put through a call. I'd used them at my last impromptu party and they'd brought their portable bar, bartenders, and booze, taking care of everything.

One more person to contact, Natasha, my favorite

tattoo artist. I absolutely had to invite her. It was time.

Jess would freak when she found out about the party and maybe rightly so. My breath caught in my throat. I didn't like screwing her around, but I couldn't keep going on the way I had. I needed this.

Having her here every day was killing me. Not that I didn't like having her around. I did. I liked it way too much. Problem was, I'd gotten used to it so quickly and what with Dad being sick, I'd let her see the real 'me'. I simply didn't work that way. Or I never had until now. A scary thing.

I'd like to see more of the real Jess too. In more ways than one. I liked what I'd seen that evening at MacMillan Martial Arts. Was it wrong to picture your bodyguard naked? I'd imagined it enough times, the toned abs, long legs, shapely hips, and those boobs, yep, I'd fantasized about them a lot.

Yet she didn't even need to put it into words. It was clear by her tone of voice and body language that nothing was going to happen between us. We'd have to see about that.

Finally ready, I picked up the Les Paul and plugged it into one of my small tweed combos. There was the Mesa Boogie stack, of course, that was way too loud to use at home but I liked having it here anyway.

So many things were dragging me down at the moment. I wanted to save my dad, for the drugs and treatment to work, and for him to live a long life.

But if I couldn't have what I wanted, I'd take something else. Guitar. Loud. Party. Hard. Drink. Lots.

CHAPTER SIX

Jess

In some ways, I couldn't believe my luck. This was absolutely the best bodyguard job I could have been assigned. Close protection usually involved long boring hours keeping watch and lots of standing around. Not here, not for me.

Instead, I was relaxing at the table while Lachie stood in the kitchen wearing an apron, an actual apron, which meant he probably wasn't trying to impress me. I tried not to dwell on that and admired the view instead. He'd tied his long blond hair back, very professional of him, even if this was the scruffiest ponytail in existence. Maybe the sexiest too.

Also, this beat the hell out of eating alone at home, not that that was always the case, but my roommate was away at the moment. Holly had been on the road a lot lately. Besides, as much as I liked her, it didn't compare with having Lachie in the kitchen.

I'd never seen him cook before and thought he might've been stressing but, no, he was as laid back as ever as he wandered to the table, a single penne on a fork in his hand.

He leaned over me, the pasta inches from my mouth. "Blow on this and tell me if you think it's ready."

My face flushed instantly. I was hungry, ready for dinner, ready for anything that might come my way. It felt strangely intimate as I pursed my lips and blew, then closed my mouth around the fork.

I chewed and swallowed. "That's *al dente*."

"Great, I'll serve up, then."

He stepped back into the kitchen, straining the pasta and scooping sauce from the pan, apparently unaware of my ridiculous reaction. Which was just as well.

The aroma of tomato and garlic intensified as he brought over the two bowls of pasta and sat down.

The first forkful exploded with flavor in my mouth. "This is sensational. I didn't know *penne arrabiata* had pancetta in it."

"Mine does." He looked proud, and rightly so.

He hadn't skimped on the spices. After a few mouthfuls, I discovered the chili had a bite to it that was building, growing on me, a bit like Lachie.

"Wow, that's got quite a kick to it," I said.

"Like you."

"You think?"

"Oh, yeah, I do."

I sipped my mineral water. "An old boyfriend of mine used to be a chef, but it wasn't like this."

Lachie laughed. "What? Are you saying I'm a better cook than him?"

It was more that Connor hadn't liked his work crossing over into his private life, which had always seemed strange to me because I figured he should be more passionate about what he did. Apparently not.

"He was my first 'real' boyfriend after I finished school." I swallowed another mouthful, wondering about Lachie. "What were you like at school? Were you some cool, stoner guitar player who the girls chased after?"

"Not a stoner but I did smoke a little weed." He shrugged. "It's not something I'm into anymore."

"I bet you were the popular guy at school."

His offhand shrug told me this meant nothing to him and perhaps when you fit in, it didn't. It was only when it was the other way around that it mattered.

I forced a smile to my face. "Different from me. I didn't have a lot of friends. I hung out with the goths."

"You were a Goth Girl?" He grinned. "You with your pretty gray eyes and your light brown hair?"

"I dyed it black, my hair, that is."

"I can't picture it," he said.

And I wasn't going to show him the photos. "My parents absolutely hated it. The loose black clothes, the eyeliner, the grungy music, it went against everything they believed in." I smiled. "Maybe that was what appealed to me so much."

That, and the fact that those kids would talk to me. I bit that last part back because Lachie didn't need to know the details.

My goth period hadn't come out of nowhere. It'd come several months after I'd been attacked on the bus. A delayed reaction, a rebellion of sorts, and I still didn't know if I'd been trying to hide or attract attention. The only thing I knew for sure was the despair I'd felt at the time.

"So tell me, Lachie Tyler, if you fit in at school and

your home life was so stable, what were you rebelling against?"

"I'm not sure if it was quite like that. I just wanted more."

"More of what?"

"Everything. My parents couldn't afford the stuff I wanted, especially as I got older. Guitars and amplifiers aren't cheap. Then there's effects pedals and loads of other things."

I knew the feeling but that wasn't what drove me. "So you thought dropping out of college and playing in a band would provide a good, safe income?"

He tilted his head. "Is that sarcasm I hear?"

"Quite possibly."

We finished eating but somehow the silence between us had an edge to it as if something was up.

I leaned back in my chair. "Is everything okay? You kept to yourself a lot today."

He shrugged. "I didn't feel like sharing my bad mood with you. And I've gotta be honest, I'm still getting used to having someone here with me all the time."

I nodded, certain he was used to having 'someone' with him much of the time, or whenever he felt like it anyway. Just not the same 'someone' all the time. A guy like him could pick and choose and move from girl to girl, and I had no doubt that was exactly what he did.

The thought sent a pang through my chest. Something I didn't want to picture, couldn't bear to think about, and thankfully hadn't had to face. But it could happen. I was kidding myself if I thought it couldn't.

Lachie reached for my empty bowl, placed it on top of his. "By the way, I'm having a few people around tonight."

I straightened, my senses alert. "Really? How many?"

"Don't know. Might be twenty or it might be two hundred."

What was he playing at? Was he even serious? I took a deep breath, refused to let him rile me.

"Sounds like a party, then," I said.

"Hope so."

Damn it, I'd wondered why he'd been so organized and diligent with the cooking when it was still only six-thirty. I should've known something was up and should never have let him lull me into this stupid sense of satisfaction.

Screw him. How selfish. And careless.

I gritted my teeth. "You can't do that. You'll have to cancel."

"No way. The party is on. I'm not changing my mind." He stood, took the dirty bowls to the kitchen.

I opened my mouth to argue but stopped myself. There was no point. He was the client and he wasn't going to listen to me anyway. There was a slim chance he might listen to Andrew. I doubted it, though.

This was way too much for me to handle on my own. At the very least, Andrew would be able to set up surveillance at the door so we could identify people coming in. We'd need guys on the perimeter of the property too. The house wasn't huge but it was big enough. My mind was racing.

Lachie hadn't thought this through or considered the repercussions. He had his eyes on me, waiting for a reaction, expecting me to jump up and down, but I refused to give him the satisfaction. Besides, I knew Andrew would blast him.

I bit back my anger. "Don't forget, in some ways Frankston is a small place."

He shrugged. "Yeah."

"And when you mix in certain circles, everyone knows everyone. Your stalker might be a friend of a friend. She might get wind of this and come along tonight."

"Not likely."

"She's closer than you think, remember?" I threw her words back at him. "We need to be prepared. A party is an uncontrolled environment, after all."

He stared across from the other side of the kitchen counter. "A party's not supposed to be controlled. It's supposed to be fun."

"I only want you to be careful."

"I am. That's why I have you. But I've got to live my life." He grabbed another beer from the fridge and left.

I took to my feet, balled my hands into fists, but it wasn't enough. Now that he'd gone, I knocked my chair to the floor and stood there shaking.

It was my job to protect him. More than a job. Damn it, I cared about him even if he didn't care nearly enough about himself.

CHAPTER SEVEN

Lachie

I was playing guitar, wasn't holding back, finally feeling free, like my old self. A transformation. And a relief. I didn't even hear the knocking or perhaps it was banging.

Jess stuck her head in the door. "People have started arriving. Nick's here."

I froze, my mouth falling open. I'd seen Jess daily, seen her at training and also out and about with me, but never like this. I had no idea a woman who was so covered up could look so sensual, so alluring, so damn good. And she wasn't even trying. She wore some long-sleeved, high-necked, lace thing that stuck to every curve and every muscle. And to the black bra underneath.

Time to put my tongue back in my mouth. She deserved better than she was getting from me. A lot better. I'd felt guilty as all hell after I'd told her about the party, but it'd been too late by then.

Nick stepped closer. "Hey, Lachie. You treating Jess to a free concert?"

She smiled, folded her arms. "I've had lots of free concerts."

"Ha! I bet you have." Nick slung his arm around me. "How's it going, dude?"

"Good." I nudged him away and put the Les Paul back on the stand, thinking I needed another beer to cool me down. And fast. "Let's go."

I locked the door behind us because I didn't want anyone getting their grubby hands on my guitars, pocketing the key at first, then changing my mind before I handed the key to Jess. "I'd better give this to a responsible adult."

"Sure."

Nick stopped halfway down the hall. "Good news. I might've found us a bass player."

That might be the best news I'd had all day. We'd put the feelers out since Austin had left the band but hadn't got very far with it. Plenty of guys were practically knocking at our door, which was part of the problem because we didn't want *them* coming to us. We wanted to search someone out ourselves. The right person.

Without a bass player, we hadn't got very far with recording the new album either. That wasn't such a big problem because there were some good session musicians around, but The Flats Festival would be a problem. We needed to have a new guy—a permanent fixture, not a temporary fix—playing with us by then.

"Who?" I asked.

"Do you remember a guy called Domino? Used to play in The Paranoid Monkeys."

"Vaguely." I remembered the band but not the bass player.

Nick motioned toward the living room ahead. "I'm gonna check on Lily. We brought Scarlett with us too."

"Excellent."

But I wasn't thinking about Nick's fiancée or her sister. I was thinking about Jess.

My hand on her lower back, I leaned in close. "I thought you were meant to be inconspicuous and fit in. You know, while you're doing the bodyguard thing."

"I take this *thing* very seriously." And she did. I could see it in her expression, her composure. "This crowd is going to be full of young women dressed to impress. I'd stand out if I looked plain and nerdy."

"You could never be nerdy."

She shot me a disbelieving look. "I might surprise you."

"You already have, Goth Girl." I reached for her hand. "There's something else. I'm sorry about being such an asshole earlier. I don't have a good excuse, just that I'm used to doing things my way."

"That's okay."

"So I *am* an asshole?"

"Not all of the time." The smile in her eyes glinted with something bordering on evil. "So how did things go with Andrew?"

"Great."

A lie. Andrew wasn't the kind of guy you fucked with. I'd been expecting his call, the choice words, the demands, so I wasn't surprised when he'd phoned. Not that it had worked. No way was I going to cancel. This was my party.

I needed a drink more than ever and ushered Jess ahead of me. We wandered into the living room where the Bar and Beyond guys had set themselves in one corner, looking very much like they were part of the furnishings.

A young woman in black pants and a white shirt must

have read my mind as she came up to me with a tray of beers. I nodded and took one.

A few people were lounging on the sofa with plenty of others standing around. I needed to relax and have a good time just for one night. Fuck the stalker. Fuck my dad's cancer. Fuck everything.

One night, that's all this was. Maybe Andrew and Nick were right about needing a bodyguard and security, after all. I had the right woman at my side. If only she'd stay here.

"You look lovely, Jess," I said. "Try to relax and enjoy yourself a little tonight. Hang with me and I can introduce you to some people so you can mingle."

She glared. "I'll be hanging close, all right. First, I've got to check how things are going at the door, then I'll be back."

I couldn't believe it. "So you're off to observe the surroundings and inspect the perimeter? Is that what you're doing?" She didn't answer so I added, "It's just a party. Nothing bad's going to happen."

"And we'll make sure it stays that way."

She had a word with one of the security guys standing nearby, motioning toward me, no doubt telling him to stick by my side.

Then she left. There was no arguing with her and probably no need for me to feel pissed off. She sure took her job seriously. Maybe she was starting to have an effect on me too because I did feel more secure knowing someone was taking care of me.

And I'd take care of the rest.

The young bartender appeared at my side. "You look like a bourbon man."

"Indeed I am."

Grinning, I swept the glass from her tray and knocked it back.

"You'll need another beer, Lachie," she said.

Definitely a mind reader. I laughed, polished off my existing beer, and took a fresh one before she left. The buzz of background noise mixed with the hum of alcohol in my gut, which was a much better feeling than earlier in the day when I'd been a cluster of nerves. I liked this much better, the sensation of being comfortably numb. In fact, that'd make a good name for a song. It made me smile.

Natasha wandered in, a case in her hand, someone I'd particularly wanted to come tonight. She was hard to miss with her black hair, red lips, and pale arms covered in tattoos. The woman loved what she did.

I greeted her with a kiss. "Glad you could make it."

"For you, Lachie, always. Do you know I had to show the guys at the door my case before they'd let me in?" She raised her finely arched brows in mock outrage. "This place is stricter than airport security."

"They didn't frisk you, did they?"

"No, but one of those guys was kind of cute."

"I'm sure he'll manhandle you later if you ask him nicely." She laughed and I added, "You can set up wherever you like."

"Maybe on the sofa. Under the lamp over there."

"Sure, but you need a drink first."

"Not while I'm working. I might grab a mineral water."

That was one of the things I liked about her. She was a professional. Also the only person I trusted to do my tattoos.

I gave her a quick hug. "I'll be back."

"Of course you will, honey."

I did the 'meet and greet' thing with some of my guests because I too was a professional. A professional party man. Also it was a good idea to do this while I was still coherent.

This was my world. I didn't even care if the security guy was following me around while I talked to people, some from local bands, a few artists who I'd known before they'd made it, some people I didn't know at all, and others like Nick who I knew very well indeed.

Not Cooper, though. He'd said he wouldn't be able to make it tonight. My gut clenched. He wasn't just our drummer. He was a good friend.

A guy I knew from school came up to talk to me, the room getting more crowded all the time, so after a while I headed outside for some air.

Looked like they'd set up a bar out here too. How handy. I helped myself, weaving my way through the small crowd that had gathered, feeling almost anonymous because it was darker out here and no one seemed to be paying me attention, which made for a nice change.

A couple of girls were relaxing in the hot tub. I had no clue why, but if there was a pool or a hot tub at a party like this, there'd always be girls taking their clothes off. There was a time I might've joined them.

One of the girls in the tub spotted me and waved. "Lachie, Lachie!"

So much for feeling anonymous for a few minutes. Her friend sat up too, both of them waving, boobs jiggling like crazy. The group next to me called out to the girls, then laughed and looked back at me, made me feel as if I was staring. And maybe I had been.

Smiling at the girls, I turned away. It wasn't that I didn't like breasts because I did. I liked them a lot, but sometimes they were a bit like a car crash where you couldn't help but stare. And it kind of made me feel like a pervert.

Then I spotted Jess nearby, talking to the security guy who'd been tailing me, hopefully getting rid of him because I'd much rather have her by my side.

A tall guy came up to me and shook my hand. "Great party. We've met before."

"Have we?"

"Joel Hitchcock." He waited, then added. "From Black Paisley." He waited some more. "The band."

"Oh, yeah, I've heard of you." I hadn't. "What do you play?"

"A bit of guitar, but bass, mostly. I can play piano if forced."

"If forced!" He made me laugh.

"And I write most of the band's songs too."

"You sound like Nick. He does a bit of everything. A good all rounder." I admired him for that and maybe it was something to admire in this guy too, whereas my love for musical instruments had never made it any further than the guitar.

"I'm more of a bass player," he said. "Didn't start off that way, but that's how it ended up."

"Why's that?"

"I'm better on bass than on guitar." He nodded in my direction, smiled a little. "I'll leave the guitar-playing to the experts."

I shrugged. "Lots of guys play bass just so they can get

a gig. Someone told me years ago that if you're a bass player, you'll always get a gig whereas everyone wants to be the guitar player. I reckon that still holds true."

After a few moments he said, "I, uh, heard you guys might be after a bass player."

What to say? He seemed like a nice enough guy, but I didn't want to talk shop right now. I wanted to drink. And party. And hang with Jess. These were the things I was good at.

"We might have already found someone," I said.

If he was trying to hide the disappointment from his face, he was failing miserably. "Really. Who's that?"

"A guy called Domino."

Lips pursed, he looked like he was holding back.

"You know him?" I asked.

"You could say that."

Scarlett came bounding up and kissed me on the cheek. Nick had already told me Lily's sister was here and she looked as beautiful as always.

"Lovely to see you again," I said.

"Wow, quite a turnout." Her brown eyes widened. "This is some house you've got."

"Thanks, I take it that's a compliment."

"You've got so much house and it's so empty."

"No way, it's full of people."

"I bet when they're all gone, this place doesn't feel like 'you'."

I grinned. "Now how do you know what I feel like?"

She laughed, turned to the guy I'd been talking to earlier, stared at him long and hard, then looked up at me expectantly. His name had left me completely. This was bad. Someone, please save me.

"Scarlett, this is…"

"Joel Hitchcock," he said.

"Yes, Joel's a bass player. With Black Paisley." At least I'd remembered the name of the band.

She turned to me. "I was hoping to talk to you … about your house. I thought you might need an interior architect, but maybe we should leave that for another time."

"Thanks for the offer but I like my place the way it is. For now, anyway. So how are things going with you?"

Her face clouded over. "Nick told me how sick your dad is. I'm so sorry to hear it, Lachie."

"That's—" I pulled myself together "—nice of you to say."

I was lucky I could get past the lump in my throat and that my voice hadn't cracked. God knows, my heart already had. My father was scheduled for surgery tomorrow and would be getting a colostomy bag. These were sometimes reversible. Not his, though. No turning back.

Still, even if all Scarlett could give me were kind thoughts, I appreciated them. So many people avoided the issue of my dad's health because it was in the too-hard-basket.

She reached for my arm. "Sorry, I didn't mean to interrupt. I just thought I should say something."

"It's okay, really, no problem at all." I raised my beer. "But tonight's not for sickness. It's for drinking."

The damn thing was empty. My cue to get another one of those Frankston IPAs. I didn't want to abandon Scarlett or Joel—he seemed like a genuine sort of guy—but I wasn't nearly drunk enough to get through the night.

Comfortably numb wasn't good enough. I wanted to be beyond numb in a place where my problems didn't exist.

And right now getting shit-faced drunk was the only way.

CHAPTER EIGHT

Jess

It wasn't often I wished I could relax like everyone else. When I'd started out in security, I'd never longed to be inside the venue drinking myself silly with everyone else and making a fool of myself in front of some guy. Standing at the door and being sober had given me a different perspective.

Tonight, instead of standing at the door I was overseeing the whole event, liaising with the guys at the front in their black bouncer outfits and others in plain clothes.

And from here on in, I'd have to stick close to Lachie. The guy drove me crazy sometimes. He wasn't taking any of this seriously, not his stalker, and not the security problems posed by this party.

We were back inside and Lachie was in party mode, deep in discussion on the sofa with Natasha, while I stood nearby. At first it had freaked me out to find a tattoo artist at the party, but I'd seen lots of weird things in my time and had gotten over it pretty quickly. Besides, I'd spoken to her earlier and she seemed to have her head screwed on.

A lull in their conversation, Natasha reached for her case.

I stepped closer. "Are you packing up?"

"No," she said. "Quite the opposite."

Lachie spread his arms. "Ah, my two favorite ladies."

Natasha pretended to be offended. "And I thought I was the only one for you. Are you ready, my man?"

"As I'll ever be." He started unbuttoning his shirt.

My heart racing, I didn't know why the thought of him getting inked made me nervous, only that it did.

"Lachie, you're drunk," I said. "Are you sure you should be doing this?"

Natasha looked up at me. "Don't worry, I don't do 'impulse tattoos'. This is a long-term project, a design I've been finessing over the last couple of months since Lachie came back to town. He didn't want to rush into anything, so here he is now."

Yep, here he was.

I held Lachie's gaze. "Are you okay?"

He nodded, emotion glimmering in his eyes. "This tattoo is going to be special."

Everyone thought their tattoos were meaningful. I did too. Unfortunately, that didn't make me feel any better.

Natasha pulled on her rubber gloves. I swallowed the lump in my throat, unable to look as Lachie lay on the sofa with Natasha kneeling on the carpet in front of him. Instead, I kept my distance, keeping watch, even though I believed the greatest threat at the moment was from Lachie himself.

It was a while until he was sitting again, buttoning up his shirt. By that stage, he looked like he needed a drink so that was exactly what he did.

After that, I stuck by him, close but not too close.

The rest of the night was uneventful, just the way I liked it. I was used to being on my feet all day—or night—but still had the chance to sit down from time to time, which made things easier for me.

By two in the morning, the living room had a few stragglers who looked like they'd settled in for the long haul and, other than that, things were winding down.

While Lachie was joking around with a group of people, a skinny guy with a shaved head pulled him aside to talk, then left.

Five minutes later, Lachie staggered up to me. "I'm heading over to my office."

"Sure."

I let him go ahead of me so I felt less like a bodyguard and more like a normal person. Also so that I could check out his butt. It was only a small treat and it wasn't as if he was in any immediate danger.

Seconds later, I stood in the doorway of his office, so called because it had a desk in it that Lachie never used. He was perched on a coffee table with his back to me, an open bottle of bourbon beside him. Three girls sat upright on a sofa opposite him, the skinny guy with the shaved head sitting on a tub chair nearby. No slouching, no chatting, it looked weird.

Deadly silence.

Lachie shrugged. "What?"

The guy on the tub chair turned white. "The table."

"What about it?"

More panicked now. "You're sitting on it."

"It's my fucking coffee table. What's the big deal?" Lachie's words were slurred but he seemed more coherent than the other guy.

Who stood, held his hands out. "Don't move. Not an inch, you hear me. You're sitting on our fucking coke."

"I'm sitting…"

The guy nodded. "On six lines of premium quality blow."

More silence.

Eventually Lachie said, "Then this is a pretty expensive pair of jeans."

The girls burst out laughing, the guy too. Though I couldn't see Lachie's face, I had no doubt he was cool as ever.

The guy with the shaved head stayed on his feet. "Careful now. I need you to stand up. Slowly."

"Okay."

The guy reached for Lachie's arm but he swatted him away. "I can stand up on my own, douche bag."

He got up gingerly, and there were indeed several lines of coke on the back of his jeans. Dropping to his knees, the guy with the shaved head picked up a rolled up bill and started snorting the remnants of the lines from the coffee table. Two of the girls got up, while the one remaining on the sofa keeled over, too drunk to stay up on her own. The first two girls crawled on the floor and started wiping the table with their index fingers, then rubbing this against their teeth and gums. Just like in the movies.

What the movies don't tell you is how pathetic this looks.

"Are you done?" Lachie sounded pissed off. "Because I need to move."

"No, no," the guy implored. "Lie down on the table very carefully on your stomach. We'll snort the lines off your ass."

The girls howled with laughter. I'd bet this would make a fantastic story for them. Not if I had anything to do with it. Anger sparked in my stomach.

Lachie wasn't a sideshow. He'd been good to these people, opened up his house, given them as much free booze as they could guzzle. And he was more than just some piece of ass.

"No, you're not." I stormed in and grabbed Lachie's shoulder. "We're out of here."

The guy with the shaved head pushed me. The last straw. I gave him a quick, sharp shunt in the chest that told him I meant business much more than his puny push had done. He stepped back, his eyes widening with shock.

"What the…?"

I glared. "Don't you dare tell Lachie what to do. Am I clear?"

He nodded, mumbled something I didn't catch.

Lachie reached for my hand and took it into his, making me feel this was all worthwhile. He leaned over and grabbed the bottle of bourbon, then let me lead him out of the room.

He stopped in the hallway and slugged back some of the booze. I once had a boyfriend who used to drink too much, a financial advisor of all things, who always miraculously sobered up by the morning. I was not going there again.

"Were you really going to let them do lines of coke off your ass?" I asked.

"Yeah, probably."

He smacked the back of his jeans with both hands, white powder floating down to the floor. My stomach sank, despair washing over me, not just because of the coke, but because he deserved better and the irony was that he was doing this to himself.

"Damn it, Lachie, I don't want you to slash and burn and end up dead in a couple of years at twenty-seven like some drugged up, fucked up rock star."

He waved it off. "I'm not gonna end up like Kurt Cobain or that Winehouse woman. I've still got a couple of years in me yet."

"But you should have so much more than that." I sucked in a deep breath to stop my voice from shaking. "Why, Lachie? Why do I have more respect for your ass than you do?"

His eyes vacant, he could barely get the words out. "I… I…"

"Oh, hell." I put my arm around him. "We'd better get you to bed."

The bourbon bottle slipped from his fingers, spilling onto the floor, so I set it upright by the wall, then stood up and let Lachie lean on me.

"Jess, Jess," he mumbled as we staggered to his room.

"What?"

No response. We made it to his bed, where he collapsed in a heap, his shoulders slumped, head hanging down. At least he could sit. That was something.

I had to put him to bed. I could handle that. Security was a different matter, something I couldn't ignore. I had to check on the remaining staff and make sure the house was safe even as people were leaving. It was my job and also the first thing I had to do if I was going to look after Lachie.

Taking his hand into mine, I gave it a squeeze. "Can

you wait five minutes for me to come back?"

Desperation in his eyes. "Don't go."

But I had to. "Don't move till I get back."

I left the room, relieved to find Andrew by the front door. He'd swung by to keep an eye on things, which was just his style and would make things a hell of a lot easier.

"I'm looking after Lachie," I said. "He's not doing so well."

"Need a hand?"

"I've got it under control."

He placed a reassuring hand on my shoulder. "You take care of Lachie. I'll check everything is secure and brief the remaining guys. Leave it to me. Rex and Harry will stay here till morning."

That was a load off my mind. I went through a couple of details with him, then grabbed a bottle of water from the fridge on my way back to the bedroom, closing the door behind me.

Lachie was slumped in exactly the same spot. I'd told him not to move. Maybe he couldn't.

I sat down, our thighs touching. Close, maybe too close. "Are you okay?"

"No."

At least he could speak. It was something. I passed him the water, watched his Adam's apple bob up and down as he drank, then took the bottle back, and placed it on the floor. Even a simple drink of water was such an effort for him.

No point mincing my words. "For crying out loud, Lachie, why do you do this to yourself? A guy like you, you've got everything going for you."

"What?"

"Why drink so much?"

"I drink—" his green eyes filled with anguish "—to forget."

"But it's not working."

"You're right." His voice cracked. "Nothing's working."

That's when it hit me. He was talking about his father's treatment. I'd spoken to him about it and had overheard enough telephone calls to know what was going on. The love and adoration in Lachie's voice when he mentioned his father came through loud and clear. And the despair.

I could hear his pain. I could feel it, along with my own pain and a spasm of jealousy because Lachie loved his parents and they loved him right back. So different from the way I'd grown up.

"Oh, Lachie."

I put my arms around him, pulling him close so his head was resting against mine. Hopefully an embrace would say what words couldn't, that I felt for him, that my heart went out to him, that I wished I could help.

He nuzzled into my neck, sending a sensual shiver up my spine, then pressed a kiss to my cheek. A platonic kiss that reminded me I shouldn't feel anything for him. I was supposed to be his bodyguard.

This wasn't what I wanted. Yet it was.

I straightened. "You need to get to bed."

He nodded.

"Can you stand?"

He got up, swaying as he stood, then dropped his jeans. The whole time I was pulling back the covers, my eyes were on the navy boxers snug against his butt. I was human after all.

Then he collapsed back onto the bed, his head landing on the pillow. Must've been down to years of practice. The guy was a pro.

Leaning over, I pulled his legs onto the bed and stretched the sheet to his hips while he lay back, peering at me, his eyes slits.

I perched myself on the bed beside him. "Your shirt has to come off too."

He fumbled with the buttons, then reached for my hand, and put it on his chest. His eyes were wide open, his words clear, as if he was suddenly more lucid.

"Can you do it?" he asked.

I swallowed. "Sure."

I unbuttoned his shirt, then pulled the sides apart, wondering how I was going to get the thing off, wondering if I should be here at all because I liked looking at that tanned, lean chest way too much. A wave of longing flooded through me, not sexual, not exactly, more like an ache. How wonderful it would be to lay my head on his chest and fall asleep in his arms, to have a different life, to be truly loved.

Instead I said, "Your new tattoo."

I shifted to the middle of the bed to get a better look, resting on one elbow while I traced my fingers carefully around the ink, avoiding the reddened skin. He had a few tats on his arms but this was the only one on his chest and that made it look more delicate, the lines flowing with ease, the script more sensual.

"Yep." Lachie was trying to say something else. It took him a while. "It's what my Dad always says."

I read the words out. "Compassion and courage."

"The two things you need to be a man."

No one was going to argue about courage. I had to agree with him about compassion too. Empathy, understanding, heart—men needed these traits as much as women.

"You're a good man, Lachie Tyler."

The tattoo made sense now. A homage to his father. And a good representation of the man before me.

I'd thought Lachie wasn't taking the important things seriously. And I'd been wrong. Because he was so much more than a guy who liked to party.

"I don't want him to die." Lachie squeezed his eyes shut, his voice strained.

My throat suddenly tight, I couldn't speak, didn't know what to say. I yearned to wrap my arms around him and hold him tight, but bit my lip to hold myself back. I couldn't throw myself at him either, not when he seemed so vulnerable.

Instead, I placed my hand on his shoulder over the shirt he was still wearing and gave it a rub. "I'm sorry, Lachie."

"Stay with me, Jess." His eyes were still closed, his expression pained.

I lay my head on the pillow beside him, keeping a modicum of distance, the comforter between us because he was under the covers and I was on top. Nerves skittered along my skin at the barrier I dared not cross. I'd gone too far already.

"Jess..."

Lachie opened his eyes, slowly bringing his hands to my face. Close, we were so close, my heart racing, skin tingling as I lay there, not daring to move.

"Jess..."

He cupped my face in his hands, his lips parted as he gazed into my eyes. He leaned closer, took his time, my heart beating faster with each passing second. Then, a beautiful moment as he brushed his lips against mine and my heart stopped. This shouldn't be happening.

"Jess..."

This time he covered my mouth with his, enveloping us in a passionate kiss. God, how I wanted this. How I was reveling in it, tears burning at the back of my eyes, tears of rapture, tears of fear, passion simmering deep inside me.

Eventually we broke off the kiss and he closed his eyes, draping one hand onto my waist in a way that made me feel delicate. I should get up. I couldn't stay here like this, yet I couldn't bear to leave.

I pushed the stray strands of hair from his face and stroked his hair, gazing at his sleeping face. I was so tired, exhausted in a way that sank deep into my core, and it was so hard to keep my eyes open. My eyelids heavy, I pulled my hand back, let it drop to his shoulder, and couldn't find the energy to take it further.

My eyes closed as I slipped gently to sleep.

CHAPTER NINE

Lachie

A lot could happen in a week. A lot had.

After the party, I'd woken up with Jess beside me but it wasn't the way I'd planned it. Wasn't like with any other girl either. It was the most beautiful, horrible experience.

Beautiful because that's the sort of person Jess was, inside and out. Horrible because I had looked and felt like shit and could barely remember what had happened. Then, as bits of the evening had come back to me, I wasn't exactly thrilled with myself. Regret flushed through me, even now.

I'd kissed her. That part was no dream. And she'd kissed me right back. She hadn't said a word about it since then and neither had I.

My life had been turned upside down again. It was the world's worst timing with Jess. My dad's surgery had taken place the following morning. They'd given him a colostomy bag, done some exploratory surgery, and removed part of his bowel and colon of several huge cancerous growths.

Huge, that was the word the doctors used.

That'd only been the beginning. He'd still been in a hospital ward recovering from his initial surgery when there were complications, a bowel obstruction that had him screaming in pain. Followed by more surgery. Which was why we'd ended up here.

And that wasn't the only thing going on, either. My stalker had been at it again too, more threatening than before. I didn't have time to deal with that shit. My dad was so much more important.

Now we were back at Franklyn General, a place I'd been to way too many times in the past. I gritted my teeth, tried to focus on Jess leaning over and washing her hands.

There were so many signs in the corridor that it felt like we were entering a nuclear missile silo or government installation. *Avoid cross contamination. Please wash your hands. Sterile area. Please respect the needs of other patients.*

And the big sign across the top of the doorway. *Intensive Care Unit.*

Jess wiped her hands on the paper towels provided, moving aside to make way for me. "It's all yours."

Squirting soap from the dispenser, I lathered up. The sign above the basin outlined the importance of washing your hands thoroughly to reduce the risk of cross infections, not that I needed reminding because the two nurses at the desk had been extremely clear.

And kind too. They'd been excited at seeing a 'rock star' but had controlled themselves from going too overboard. As much as I hated the label, this was one of those times when fame came in handy. They had rules about everything in this place—only immediate family allowed and no more than two visitors at a time among them—but the nurses had said Jess could come in with me. I wanted her at my side when I saw my mom and dad.

I turned to Jess and motioned toward the ICU. She seemed to understand I didn't want to speak as we headed down the corridor. I stopped outside the door, took a deep breath.

Courage and compassion, I was going to need both of those traits. Taking Jess's hand into mine, I pushed the door open with my free hand, pulling her behind me. She gave me strength just be being there.

Dad was propped up in the middle bed, one of five, with Mom sitting beside him. Because there was nowhere else she'd be.

My breath caught in my throat at the sight of them. They shouldn't be here. This shouldn't be happening.

Pulling Jess along behind me, I dropped her hand as we got closer. My folks had met her before, and I didn't want to explain anything else about the relationship, especially since there was nothing between me and Jess, not really. Not yet.

Mom turned, jumping to her feet to give me a big hug. She felt small in my arms. Frail. Surely she hadn't felt this way the last time I hugged her.

After that, she and Jess said hello to each other, but I couldn't get my eyes off my dad. My heart lurched in my chest. A couple of weeks ago, he'd seemed to be a regular guy. Now he looked like an old man, when he wasn't even sixty yet. Worn out.

"Dad, so good to see you." My voice cracked, something I'd have to watch because I didn't want to upset him.

I leaned over and hugged him. As I stood, he kept one hand on my forearm, the closest he could get to reciprocating.

"You're getting stronger," he said.

"Dad, I'm not eight years old anymore."

"And I'm not dead yet so don't you go looking at me like that."

It was taking all his energy to put on a brave face. I could see it in his face and the tendons straining in his neck. I bit back my own pain, forced myself to keep things light just the way Dad would like them.

I cleared my throat. "Seems your vocal cords are working just fine."

"Sure are." Then to Jess, "Hello over there."

"Nice to see you again," she said.

"You don't know that yet. I might be in a bad mood."

Mom sat back down on the chair. "Pete, you're supposed to be resting."

"Of course I'm resting." Dad sounded indignant. "I'm lying down, aren't I?"

I forced a smile to my face. "Sounds like we've got the same grumpy old man back, then."

I only wished it were true. Jess stepped back and started scanning the room, a habit of hers. She was leaving us to it, which was considerate.

We were so damn grateful simply to have Dad here. The doctors had said that at one point during surgery his heart had stopped and it was touch and go. *Touch and go.* The words had cut right through me.

"You know what the worst thing is?" My father's voice was strained.

I raised my eyebrows. "No, but I'm sure you're going to tell me."

"The worst thing about a colostomy bag is finding the

shoes to match!" Dad pressed his eyes shut, struggling to get the words out but determined.

"I bet you've been saving that one." Mom had a look on her face that told me she'd heard it all before.

Jess smiled wanly from the other side of the room.

His eyes still squeezed shut, a strange guttural sound escaped my father's lips and he clutched his abdomen with both hands, his face contorted in pain.

Mom got up, her hand on his shoulder to console him, a different sort of pain in her face.

I rushed to the nurses' station, pointing to my dad. "Something's wrong."

The nurse, a big African America guy, came over right away. He checked Dad's pulse and asked several questions, all of which took Dad a while to answer. My gut clenched in fear, I stepped back and watched, left them to it because there was nothing I could do to help. It wasn't long till Dad got a bit of color back in his face and opened his eyes again.

"So the pain has passed?" the nurse asked.

"Yes," Dad croaked.

"I think you may have overdone it. You need complete bed rest. You can exert yourself just by talking too much, you know."

Dad nodded and didn't argue for a change.

I thanked the nurse as he left, glad someone was taking control of the situation. Mom came closer and pressed a kiss to Dad's lips, then stroked his hair, speaking to him in hushed tones. He mumbled a few words back.

My jaw tight, I clenched my teeth. It pained me to see them like this. The two of them should be going to work, taking walks, and pottering around the house on weekends, planning their next vacation, not hanging around a goddamn hospital ward. Not even a regular room. The ICU.

I turned to see Jess still behind me. Stepping closer, I gave her a grim smile.

"Let me know if I can do anything," she whispered.

"It's enough that you're here," I said. "It means a lot to me."

Which was true. I felt less alone knowing there was someone I could turn to.

After a while, I went over to my parents. "Dad, are you feeling a bit better?"

He nodded.

"Mom, when was the last time you had something to eat?"

No answer.

"I knew it," I said. "You're as bad as Dad. You need to look after yourself too."

She looked down. "Maybe you're right."

"You should go and get a coffee and something to eat." I took her hand, pulled her away from the bed. "I'm here, so there's no problem with you getting away for a bit. You've got to eat."

Mom glanced at Jess and didn't say anything.

Jess smiled weakly. "He's right."

"Okay," Mom said. "Honey, it's just…"

"What?"

She bit her lip. "You've done so much for us already."

I didn't care about the money. The medical intervention wasn't working, that was the part I cared about, the bit that left me gutted.

Besides, what kind of son would I be if I didn't help

them out when they needed it? What kind of person?

I squeezed her hand. "You've got it the wrong way around, Mom. You and Dad are the ones who've done everything for me."

"Your dad loves having you here. You know that, don't you?"

"And you know where the coffee shop is, don't you?"

She smiled wanly. "Sounds as if you're trying to get rid of me."

"Absolutely." I turned to Jess. "Would you mind keeping an eye on my mom?"

She hesitated, didn't say anything in front of my parents, and shook her head instead.

The furrow in her brow gave me a pretty good idea what was going on in her head. She didn't want to leave my side at the best of times and certainly not after the latest message from my stalker.

God told me not to shoot you in the back, my darling. You'll see your angel face-to-face.

A shiver shot up my spine at the thought, but I was damned if I'd let a stalker, some coward hiding behind the internet, rule my life.

"I insist, Jess." No response. There was only one way to make her go, so I added, "That's an order, soldier."

"Sure," she said eventually.

"Lachie." Dad opened his eyes, looked at me. "Stay."

I went to him, took his hand into mine. "I'm staying, Dad. That's the plan."

If all I could do was hold my dad's hand, then that was what I would do. I wasn't going anywhere.

CHAPTER TEN

Jess

Lachie's mom unwrapped the chicken sandwich, held it in her hands. "It seems that just as soon as we get over one hurdle, something else happens."

I sipped my coffee. "Lachie has told me a bit about Pete's illness and what you've been through."

Julie looked around the café. "To think, we thought we'd left this all behind us."

"Hopefully, Pete's getting through this and you'll be leaving it in the past."

She stopped part way through her sandwich. "So tell me about this stalker business."

That'd come out of nowhere. Or perhaps not quite. The expression on her face told me she'd been thinking about this.

So that was why she'd agreed to take a break. Clever woman.

Time to change the subject. "The coffee's good. Much better than I'd have expected. You should try it."

"I know. I've been here before. Now tell me about Lachie and the stalker."

"Honestly, I think you've got enough on your plate without worrying about him too."

She chewed, gave me a dull look. "I'm his mother. I worked out a long time ago that I'm going to be worrying about him for the rest of my life. Doesn't matter how successful he is or how old, that's just how it is."

A pang shot through my heart because my own mother would never say those words or have those sorts of feelings. I'd always told myself she loved me but now I wasn't so sure. She didn't worry about me and certainly hadn't had any second thoughts when she'd left me with my aunt and uncle at sixteen. I'd only been a kid. A lonely kid at that.

I stared into Julie's eyes. How wonderful it must be to have someone who loved you that way.

"Lachie's safe," I said. "That's the main thing."

"Please don't think I can't handle it because I can. I'd rather know the truth."

"Okay, so far the stalker is only making threats." I spoke slowly, chose my words carefully. "There are a lot of weirdos around and one of them has latched onto Lachie. It doesn't mean this person will get violent. And I'm only here as a precautionary measure in case the situation worsens or in case something goes wrong, but that doesn't mean anything will."

"Normal people don't have bodyguards."

"True, but Lachie's life isn't exactly normal."

"You've got a point." She leaned back, stared at the remaining half of the sandwich sitting in front of her. "Maybe I'm using Lachie as a distraction. So I don't worry about Pete so much."

"Maybe."

"I want the best for my son. You said yourself his life isn't normal." She shook her head. "I don't know why he doesn't just find himself a nice girl, someone he can take care of, and who'll take care of him. That's all it comes down to in the end."

I swallowed the lump in my throat along with a mouthful of coffee. "Sorry, Lachie's private life isn't any of my business."

Or it shouldn't be. The way he'd kissed me that night came back to me. If only the kiss meant as much to him as it did to me. If only it meant something.

Damn it, I shouldn't even be thinking about that and sure as hell shouldn't be wallowing in the memory, but I did. Way too much.

Julie leaned forward, lips pursed. "He'd tell me it's not my business too. But I'm allowed to have my opinions. And in my humble opinion, he's attracted to the wrong sorts of girls. You know the sort. Big boobs, lots of long blond hair, way too much makeup." She held my gaze, then added, "You don't wear too much makeup. You're not wearing any at all. And you look lovely with your hair pulled back. It shows off your features."

"Thanks, ma'am. There's a reason for that. I'm working."

She stood, couldn't quite keep the smile from her face. "Don't you *ma'am* me."

"You're right, Julie. We should get going." I got up, placing our three take-out cups in the cardboard coffee cup holder. I'd ordered an extra one for Lachie. "You should wrap up the rest of your sandwich. For later."

"Good thinking." She took the sandwich with her.

I held the door open for her as we left, heading for the

elevator. My normal walking pace verged on speed walking, whereas Julie didn't seem to have the energy to hurry along, and I couldn't blame her.

She pressed the button for the elevator. "What about you, Jess? Do you have someone waiting for you at home?"

My face flushed. "I've got a roommate."

"That's not what I meant."

I stepped into the elevator. "Things are pretty quiet on the boyfriend front."

Julie got in, the doors closing behind her. "No, I didn't think there'd be many men willing to wait patiently at home while you were with a famous guitar player 24/7."

"Maybe not."

It wasn't something I'd given a lot of thought and this wasn't a position I'd been in before. But his fame had attracted a stalker, and was the very reason I was here. I couldn't forget it.

We stepped out of the elevator, heading down the long corridor that led to the ICU.

"Lachie's not the way he seems," Julie said quietly.

"Sorry?"

"He's a sensitive soul and feels much more than he'd ever let on."

Which was true. Underneath he sparkled, shone like the brightest star in the sky, and he didn't want anyone else to know, which only made him all the more endearing.

As we passed the ICU counter, we smiled at the same nurses who'd seen us leave earlier, then took turns washing our hands before heading into the Intensive Care Unit.

Nothing had changed. The same patients were there and Lachie was still by his father's side. He took the coffee cup holder from his mom and placed it on the tray beside the bed.

"Only half a sandwich, Mom?"

She nodded. "I'm saving the rest for later."

"Dad's asleep."

"I'm glad he's resting." She tilted her head, gazing first at her husband and then at her son. "You might as well go, honey. There's no point in you hanging around. I'll stay."

He pulled his mom close, wrapped his arms around her, her head pressed against his chest.

She broke off the embrace. "Love you, Lachie."

"Love you too, Mom."

Such simple words. When was the last time I'd heard them? It took my breath away.

"We should get going," he said to me.

"Do you want to take your coffee with you?" I asked.

He shook his head. "But thanks for thinking of me."

We said goodbye to his mom, then headed back down the corridor.

At the elevator, Lachie pressed the 'up' button. "We're not going straight home. We're making a detour."

I stepped inside. "Where to?"

"You'll see."

The doors closed behind us. I didn't like playing games but I also had to accept the way Lachie worked. Besides, we were in a hospital, not exactly a high-danger zone.

We strode down the corridor. According to the signage, we were either headed for Radiology or the Adolescent Unit. We walked straight past Radiology so that answered that question.

"Do you know someone here?" I asked.

"Not really."

"How do you know the way?"

"I've been here before."

I decided to give up on the twenty questions. We walked through the doorway toward the Adolescent Unit counter, proudly painted in lime green with a purple wall behind it. I approved. The place still smelled like a hospital but there was no reason it should look like one.

"Lachie!" One of the nurses looked up from the counter. About the same age as his mom, she was beaming from ear to ear. It seemed he had an effect on women of all ages.

"Hi, Michelle," he said.

"Look, it's Lachie." She nudged the other nurse, then put her hand on her hip. "So nice to see you again."

"Yep, it's me. This is Jess, by the way."

"Hi, Jess."

I smiled in response.

"I didn't bring any merchandise with me this time," Lachie said. "I hope that's okay. I can come back with more gear next time."

"Did you want to have a wander around?" the nurse asked. "I'll show you through to the ward."

She slipped out from behind the counter, smiling and chatting as we ambled closer to the ward.

"Okay." She stopped inside the doorway of a room where four girls were sitting up in bed. "Has anyone here heard of The Merchants of Menace? Because I have one heck of a surprise for you." The nurse couldn't stop smiling.

Lachie stepped inside. "Um, hi, guys."

One of the girls looked like she was about to faint while another shouted, "Oh my god, that's Lachie Tyler."

"I'll leave you to it." The nurse left.

I followed Lachie into the room. Such a shame they hadn't extended the bright color scheme this far, instead, leaving the room in shades of beige and white.

But the girls' faces were bright and bursting. Even the girl who'd appeared faint was grinning, her eyes wide. It made me feel ready to burst too, in the best way possible.

The OMG girl looked ready to jump out of bed so Lachie went to her first.

"How are you doing?" he asked.

"Lachie, can I have a photo, please, please, please?"

He smiled right back at her. "Sure you can."

She was instantly beaming, fussing over her hair, and smiling for the photo. "You've made my day. Made my whole life." A hand on her chest, she added, "I can't believe this."

As we made our way through the ward, Lachie was easygoing and at ease with everyone, chatting to them, asking them about themselves and listening. That was what got to me. He was actually listening.

There were plenty of fans there, a couple who'd never heard of the band or didn't care, and several who simply said what they thought. One very serious young girl thought The Merchants first album was by far their best and hoped this downward spiral wouldn't continue. Another said she only listened to Christian music. And all of it was fine by Lachie.

The boys' ward was on the other side of the reception counter so we made our way over there too. I didn't say much, just left Lachie to it because he clearly knew what he was doing.

After a while he said, "I'll just talk to this one last kid

and then we'll go."

I nodded. "Sure."

The boy was sitting up in bed, his brown eyes wide, skin that may have once been olive looking faded, his smooth scalp devoid of hair. It sent a pang through my heart. The poor boy should've been going to school, playing baseball and chasing girls, not sitting in a hospital bed.

"Hi, I'm Lachie."

"I knoooow." The look on the kid's face said it all. "I'm a fan, like, a really big fan."

Lachie shook the boy's hand. "Pleased to meet you…"

"Brandon."

"So, Brandon, what brings you here?"

"To the hospital? Cancer."

Lachie perched on the edge of the bed. "Same reason I'm here, then. Not that I'm sick but my dad has cancer. He's in the ICU."

"Oh." A pause. "He must be really sick."

"Yeah, but that's another story. I want to know about *you*. What do you do when you're not stuck in hospital?"

A shy smile crept to his face. "I play guitar."

"Really? That's awesome."

"And you're kind of one of the reasons I took up guitar."

Lachie grinned. "No way, really?"

"And the other reason is a really old band my dad likes, The Pixies. Have you heard of them?"

"You're a Pixies fan? You won't believe this but my dad put me onto them too. Do you like their new stuff as well?"

"I'm not sure. I haven't heard the new albums."

"Then I'll get you some CDs because you've got to listen to *Indie Cindy* and *Head Carrier*. They're killer albums and I've got to bring you up to the times, my man." Lachie raised his eyebrows. "We played on the same bill as them once. Now that was something. They're amazing live too."

I sighed. "They're not coming for the Flats Festival or I'd get you tickets."

Brandon's eyes were about to pop out. "You would?"

"I'll get you tickets anyway."

"Ohhh, that'd be fantastic." He paused, thoughtful. "When I get home I'm going to write some new songs. I'm feeling so inspired just talking to you."

"You write your own stuff?"

He nodded. "I'm not as good as you or Nick, but I'm not so bad."

Lachie gave him a fist bump. "Go, Brandon."

My heart in my mouth, I watched as they chatted and Lachie told him he'd come back soon. This was a side of Lachie I hadn't seen before, a part of his character I'd bet not many people had seen, one aspect of him that was soft and generous and as far from that of a rock star as you could get.

What's more, Lachie was a natural at this ... because he was Lachie.

As we got into the elevator, he said, "Man, that sucks."

I didn't say anything.

He added, "This is one fucked up world when kids like him get cancer."

"Yeah, it is."

I could have sworn there were tears in his eyes. My heart melted. I wanted to reach out and hold him, smother him in kisses, never let him go. I wanted to make all the bad things in the world go away, which was probably what he wanted too.

At the same time blood was surging through my veins, making me feel alive, and I had a horrible feeling I knew what was happening.

I'd gone too far. I was falling in love and there was nothing I could do about it.

This was wrong in so many ways I didn't know where to start. As a bodyguard, this was the last thing that should be happening. It could compromise Lachie's safety if I took my eye off the ball even for a second. This wasn't a joke.

Besides, Lachie didn't love me. He didn't feel for me. Desperation clawed away inside me because it wasn't supposed to happen this way. Wasn't supposed to happen at all.

Still, I couldn't bear to see him in pain, so I said, "Brandon will love the CDs and tickets. That was very thoughtful of you."

"I can make 'em feel better for all of about five minutes but I can't change anything. The doctors and medical staff are the ones performing the real miracles, not me."

"Don't be so hard on yourself. You might not be saving their lives but you're making a difference."

We stepped out of the elevator and strode outside into the sunshine. I kept my eye out as we paid for our ticket, then walked through the parking lot. I had to be constantly aware of our situation and environment.

I drove Lachie's car back to his place. The whole time I tried to drum it through my head—*don't fall in love, don't fall in love.* My heart kept racing.

Because it was too late, way too late. How could I have let this happen?

"Thanks for coming to the hospital with me," Lachie said.

As if I was doing him a favor, as if he'd forgotten I was being paid for this. I didn't need to be reminded this was my job, but the truth was I'd have been here for him anyway.

He turned to me in the driver's seat. "You don't talk much about your own family."

"There's not that much to say."

"That's not really fair since you know all about mine."

I slowed down for a kid on a bike ahead of me. "I'm an only child, so there was just me and my mom and dad. My parents moved away, and I have an aunt and uncle I see all the time."

"You make it sound simple."

"It wasn't."

The words slipped out before I could stop them. We were here. I reached for the remote, unlocking the gate, then drove in.

I saw the package on the front porch before we were out of the car. Not a package, a gift bag, metallic silver like you could buy from any drug store.

A quick scan of the area around confirmed what I thought when we'd driven in. No one around. My pulse quickened, senses alert.

Nudging Lachie to one side, I glanced down at the contents of the gift bag. The stalker was getting closer. We were entering a new phase. I felt it in my gut.

I scooped the bag up by its cord handle, unlocking the door with the keys in my other hand. The cops wouldn't be able to get prints off the cord anyway and I wanted us both safely inside as quickly as possible. Lachie didn't argue. Went straight in.

"I'll call Andrew," I said. "I'll do a sweep of the house before you go any further."

"What's in the bag?"

"We'll call the police too, of course."

"What's in the bag, Jess?"

Lachie didn't deserve this. He had enough on his plate with his family and everything else going on in his life. And now his stalker was crossing another line.

I held his gaze. "Bullet cartridges."

He didn't say anything, just stared, his lips thin, eyes narrowing.

This was exactly why I had to be on my guard.

CHAPTER ELEVEN

Lachie

"You have to come and see this." It was Nick on the other end of the phone. "It's right up your alley, an original '58 White Falcon."

Though I'd always thought of myself as a Gibson Man, I had a thing about the Gretsch White Falcon. Besides, just because I owned a beautiful Les Paul didn't mean I couldn't lust after other guitars. They weren't like women. It was okay to have more than one at a time.

Besides, Nick knew me too well. In San Francisco, I'd already passed on '57 White Falcon because it had DeArmond pickups, and '58 was the first year they moved to Filter'Trons. Nick was a guitar nerd too, though maybe not as much as me.

"At Charlie's?" I asked.

"That's where I am right now. I'll wait for you."

I drummed my fingers on my thigh. One thing was for sure, stalker or no stalker, I was not staying holed up like a prisoner in my own house. I was fed up with the whole thing, with talking to Andrew, and with explaining myself to the police when I'd done nothing wrong.

Not with Jess, though. I wasn't fed up with her.

Screw the stalker. I still had a life to live, and it wasn't as though I was going to do anything stupid. Visiting the local music store was like breathing and eating. It had to be done, especially since we were talking about a White Falcon.

"I'll be there." I hung up the phone.

There was a time I could jump in the car and drive myself to Charlie's Guitars and Records or anywhere else for that matter, when I could call people up for a party and get rotten drunk, when I could do what I wanted. Those days were over.

Jess would be good about it, though. She'd make arrangements and take precautions and drive me.

I needed her more than I wanted to admit. I liked having her around. More than liked it. Something had shifted between us in the last few days, ever since that first trip to the hospital to see my dad. Which was also the same day we found the bullet cartridges.

And I didn't like the distance between us.

I needed a distraction. And my life back again.

*　　*　　*

Walking into Charlie's was like coming home all over again. This wasn't the first time I'd been here since The Merchants had been back but somehow I was seeing it with fresh eyes. And feeling it too.

Guitars hung from the wall in rows, three high, amps stacked up in front of them and by the walls. Nearby, a couple of guys on stools were facing each other, playing acoustic. I could swear the smell of spruce and cedar was wafting through the air. One of the staff was showing a family around, and guitar was blaring from the supposedly soundproof room down the back.

I sighed. My idea of heaven. I'd been to music stores around the world but there was only one Charlie's.

Jess placed her hand on my shoulder, ushering me ahead, probably because she didn't like me standing near the doorway, too open, too dangerous. Funny how her hand felt so little, yet she made me feel secure. And something else too.

I liked her hands on me. I felt close to her in a way I couldn't explain. A connection I couldn't quite identify. And I spent way too much time thinking about her hands all over me, imagining peeling off her clothes and exploring every square inch of her body. Because I wanted to be close to her in every way.

She nodded to a guy in a black T-shirt near the counter, one of Andrew's guys, no doubt. It brought me back down to earth. After hanging out with Jess, I was getting good at spotting this stuff. Andrew would be here soon too. To see the guitar, he'd said.

We'd parked in the back. Didn't matter about the size of the car, Jess had reversed into a tight spot like a pro. She'd checked out the parking situation on Google before we'd left. When I'd asked her what she was doing, she'd said there shouldn't be a problem because there were two ways in and out of the parking lot so we couldn't get blocked in.

I was glad she was looking out for me, truly I was. That didn't change the fact I wished she was more interested in me in other ways.

"Hiya, dude." Nick came up to us, giving me a fist bump and Jess a kiss on the cheek. I felt a stab of resentment, maybe even jealousy. A friendly kiss, yes, but how come he was the one who could kiss her? And put a smile on her face, no less.

I refused to let it bug me. "Hey, thanks for calling me."

"How's the little fella, Nick?" Jess always asked about his boy even though she'd never met Thomas.

"He's as gorgeous as always. He's talking about playing guitar. Like Daddy."

I raised my eyebrows. "So has 'Daddy' bought him a guitar?"

"A toy one," Nick said. "I mean, he's only four. Can't let him go putting his sticky fingers on my guitars."

"Sticky Fingers. Hey, that'd be a good name for an album."

He smiled. "Shame we can't use it. Anyway, we've got to record the damn record first."

And we had to finish writing the songs. Man, I had so much on my mind, I'd barely given that any consideration lately. Songs didn't come out of thin air. Well, sometimes they did, but mostly they came out of a process. Called songwriting, surprisingly enough.

Three wide steps acted as a room divider between the guitars on the lower level and the CDs and records on the other side. Two boys of about thirteen or fourteen were staring and pointing.

I'd been around their age when Dad had brought me here to buy my first guitar, a used yellowing-blond Telecaster I still couldn't bear to part with. My folks had never been loaded but Dad could see I was serious about guitar and had got me the best instrument he possibly could.

I swallowed the lump in my throat, tried to think positive.

The two kids whispered and conferred, then ambled over, eyes wide. Nick and I kept talking but we both knew what was coming.

"Hi, I'm a huge fan," the taller of the two boys said. Taller and skinnier with more zits.

"Joey works for the school paper," the other one said.

Joey elbowed him in the ribs. "It's a blog." Then to me and Nick. "Can I interview you for the official school blog? Please. Would that be okay?"

"Which school?" I asked.

"Wilson High."

I nudged Nick. "Our old school. But, sorry, boys, we're looking at guitars and don't have time for an interview."

Disappointment in his face, then he brightened. "Would it be okay if we took some photos and documented the visit? We won't get in your way. We promise."

The kid stared at me with eyes that were big and hopeful and touched my heart. Or they would have if I was that sort of guy.

I nodded. "You go ahead and document it all you like."

Nick and I stepped away while Jess had a word to them. Sometimes I couldn't get my eyes off her. She was so composed, so genuine with the boys, so fluid. That was the word for her. She flowed from situation to situation and morphed into whatever was required, yet at the same time she was still always Jess.

I didn't even see the White Falcon until Nick pulled it off the wall. Only to be blown away. I'd never believed in love at first sight. I did now.

Taking it from his hands, I held the guitar at arm's length, drinking in its beauty. I'd seen amazing guitars before and had even played a $300,000 Les Paul Sunburst at a store in New York, but none had left me dripping with desire.

"Do you like it?" Nick asked.

Dumb question. "I love it."

"Gretsch used the sparkle drum coverings for the bindings."

And he insisted he wasn't a guitar nerd. "Yeah, I read that."

Looking more closely, I saw the sparkle binding was in remarkable condition for its age. I even liked the crack in the scratch plate. Character, personality, this baby was overflowing with the stuff. And I loved how the gold had worn off the pickups and hardware. Another sign of the life it had lived.

I put my foot up on a small amp so I could rest the guitar on my leg and played a couple of chords. I even liked the feeling of the guitar resonating against my chest.

Nick picked up an acoustic, sat on a nearby stool, and started strumming.

"Are you tempted by anything here?" I asked.

"Nope, not until I get a Nick Steel signature model."

I grinned. "You'll be waiting a while."

The guy had nearly everything, except this one thing he coveted, a guitar in his name. I'd mentioned it to a Gibson representative once, but nothing had come of it. Some things were out of our control.

Meanwhile, Nick got louder on the guitar. A group of people came down the steps from the record store to listen while others from the guitar section gathered around.

Several took out their phones and started recording.

Charlie came up and whacked me on the back.

"You'll need one of these." He added a guitar strap to the Gretsch and plugged me into an amp, a ratty-looking Tweed Pro to be exact, while I got ready.

"It's a '58," he said. "Same age as the guitar."

I strummed. Smiled. Couldn't get the grin off my face. "Man, this really chimes."

The sound wasn't just bright, it was so much warmer than I was expecting. It was everything I could want in a guitar.

Charlie left us to it. Maybe it was the guitar or the vibe or the room filling up with people, but I felt like channeling my inner Brian Setzer so I started playing an old Stray Cats number that Nick and I used to do back when we were at school.

Somehow rockabilly made me think of Austin, which sent a pang through my chest because he'd left the band, let us all down.

Time to turn things around. We didn't normally play covers anyway. I strummed the opening chords of *Always at Midnight*, one of the first songs I'd written for The Merchants.

Nick joined in, doing what he did best. Performing. The crowd clapped.

After another couple of songs, I searched for the two school kids.

"Hey, everyone," I called out. "Where are the two young dudes we were talking to earlier? Are you guys still here?"

Two skinny arms went up from within the crowd.

"Excuse me, folks, can you please make way for these

two young men." Grinning, I added, "They're documenting this for their school blog."

This got a good reaction from the crowd as people at the front made way for the two kids who had the biggest smiles on their faces. They looked the way I felt. Like a million dollars.

My eyes landed on Jess, standing next to Andrew near the door. She wasn't doing anything, just standing there, yet the strangest yearning grabbed hold of me—to take her home, to keep her at my side all the time, to make her a part of my life.

It wasn't merely lust, though there was plenty of that. It was something deeper, more insidious, something taking over inside. It hadn't happened at first sight but it had definitely happened.

I didn't even try to deny it. I went along with the flow. Suddenly I realized all eyes in the room were on me. I had to do something, and quick.

Sucking in a deep breath, I leant over to turn up the amp. "Okay, let's see if this thing goes to eleven."

Whooping from the crowd. Cheers. Yelling. No wonder I loved this stuff so much. No wonder I was ... in love.

I'd have thought a realization like this would make me panic. Instead, it made me search for Jess in the crowd again. She smiled. So serene. Warmth flooded through me.

I wasn't a rock star but I was still two people—a guy in a band and someone else, who was just a guy. And Jess was there in both worlds, bringing them together, keeping me sane and whole.

It was if the guitar started playing itself as the chords of the next song rang out, my fingers, my mind, all of me on automatic. Without even knowing it, I was playing *Love like Eternity*, a song I'd written expressing my deepest desires.

I kept looking at Jess. Couldn't help it. And she kept scanning the room. She was here for a reason, doing her job. I wasn't going to leave it at that, though, no way. I was two guys and neither of them were the kind of person to take no for an answer.

The song finished and the crowd clapped, the buzzing inside me increasing. There was something about playing in front of an audience that was like riding a wave.

I put my hand up. "Thanks, everybody. Hope we haven't made too much noise for you."

Whoops and yelling. "More, more!"

There weren't that many people, but they were making a hell of a noise so we played another song. Nick wasn't quite done either. I could see it in his posture so it was good for him to get this out of his system and then finish on a high note.

He stood, waved, and took a bow. What a guy. I unplugged the guitar, making it clear this was over.

The crowd started to move away. I figured people had called their friends or put the message out on social media which was why the place had filled up in the first place. They were here for the show and probably weren't going to hang around and buy a guitar.

But I was.

Charlie was standing behind the counter, his arms spread out, watching me like he knew what was coming. I walked up and placed the guitar on the counter.

He raised his eyebrows. "You'll be needing the case for that then?"

"What makes you so sure I'm buying it?"

"The look on your face."

I laughed. "Maybe I can't afford it."

"You're not going to try and haggle, are you?"

Of course, I was going to haggle so that was exactly what I did. It was a matter of principle and had nothing to do with how much money I had. After a bit of going back and forth, we agreed on an amount.

Charlie was wiping the guitar with a cloth, putting it back in the case, when Jess came up. He took off the price tag, placed it on the counter.

Jess's mouth formed a perfectly shaped O.

"Yeah, it's a lot of money," I said.

"That thing is worth more than my car."

"It's a '58. Probably older than your car too."

"Sure is."

I glanced across the other side of the counter. "Do you know Charlie here wasn't even going to give me a discount? Daylight robbery, some would call it."

He smiled. "You should have more respect for your elders."

We chewed the fat, made a couple of jokes about his age, then I lifted the guitar case from the counter. My new baby.

I turned to Jess. "We should go visit my dad. I can show him the guitar. He'd like that."

She nodded as we walked toward the door. "That shouldn't be a problem."

I put my arm around her. "You know, everything we do seems to be all about me."

"Because you're the client. You're the one I'm looking after."

"I don't want it to be that way."

It felt right to have my arm around her but it didn't last long.

She stopped, gazed at me. "Look, I'm sorry you've got a stalker but you need to be patient for a little longer."

I wasn't going to let this go. "Maybe we could visit your family some time, see how they're doing."

"Huh? Where'd that come from?"

"You said you had an aunt and uncle here in town. It'd be a nice, safe activity. I'm sure there's no stalker at their house."

"Doesn't that seem kind of weird?"

"No." Not when I wanted to get to know her.

A shy smile on Jess's face. "Actually, my aunt is a bit of a fan."

"That'll work out nicely then." I looked across at Andrew standing by the door. "Any reason he's waiting around?"

"You know the drill. The greatest likelihood of attack is when someone is getting in and out of the car. He's just keeping an eye out, that's all. It'd be stupid not to make the most of his presence while he's here."

Which made me feel like a little kid being baby sat. Or worse, a spoilt rock star.

I liked Andrew. I just didn't want him to be around more than he needed to. I was doing just fine with Jess at my side.

"It's a precaution and doesn't mean anything is wrong," Jess said, perhaps mistaking the look on my face for fear.

I gritted my teeth. "No problem."

Not surprisingly, there were no stalkers or attackers

out on the street or down the lane as we made our way down the side of the building. One of Andrew's guys stood at the edge of the parking lot, shaking his head and motioning.

When we reached the edge of the lot, Andrew put a hand on my chest. "Stay here."

Like hell I was going to stand there. It wasn't as though the place was filled with crazed gunmen. And that was my car.

The driver's window was smashed in, glass on the ground. Anger burned inside me, a small ember at first, growing with each breath. How dare they.

Andrew held a hand out. "Don't touch the vehicle."

Now he sounded like a cop. Jess unlocked the car with the remote while Andrew took a handkerchief from his pocket, presumably so he wouldn't leave prints, and opened the doors. Who even carried a handkerchief anyway?

I took a deep breath, put the guitar down, tried to compose myself. It was only a car, only the window, and nothing to worry about. Didn't stop me from being pissed off, though.

"Any idea who might break into your car?" Andrew asked, even though we both knew the answer. I didn't say anything so he added, "Has anything been taken?"

"There wasn't anything in there to start with."

Jess pointed to the back seat, her other arm in front of me, holding me back. "Andrew."

"Oh, shit." He leaned closer to check, then moved back.

I could see it clearly now, actual shit on the back seat. Disgust curdled in my stomach. I turned away, even though I couldn't smell it from here, then turned back, couldn't stop staring.

"Someone shat in my car." I balled my free hand into a fist.

Jess stepped in front, her arm spread across my chest to hold me back. Despite my anger, I liked having her close, feeling her body against mine. I just wished it didn't have to be this way.

"I know it seems gross," she said.

"You're telling me."

"But I've seen this before. It's a natural response to fear—part of the fight or flight reflex. It has an effect on the sphincter muscles. That's probably why the person defecated in your car."

Great, just what I needed to hear. "How do you even know this shit?"

I held a hand out. I didn't want to make the bad pun and didn't want an answer because I wasn't going to understand why someone would choose to break into my car and then freak out so much that they lost control of their bodily functions.

I stepped back, taking Jess's hand into mine because now that she was close, I didn't want to let her go.

"I'll have the car professionally cleaned," I muttered.

"Not yet, you can't." Andrew's voice. Somehow I didn't like the sound of this anymore, as he added, "We'll call the police. They'll want to do forensic testing as well as check the car for prints and run those against their records."

"Can we borrow your car?" Jess asked Andrew.

He handed her the keys. She opened the trunk so I could put my new guitar in there and we got into his SUV which was parked next to mine. I knew the way Jess worked. She'd want to get me home safely.

She started the engine. "When you and Nick did your impromptu set in there, did you notice anything strange, someone who seemed out of place, in particular a female, anyone who was staring?"

"Everyone was staring." Which was true. That'd been the whole point.

"No one followed us here, I'm sure of it. More likely this person heard you guys were here from a friend or maybe from social media. Everyone inside was on their phones. A couple were live streaming."

How cool for them that they could walk into a guitar store and watch a gig for free. Some of those people would be on a high for the rest of the day and all of them would be talking about it.

And how wonderful for me and Nick that we could do our thing and give people pleasure. How fantastic that I could buy the guitar of my dreams without stressing about the money because not many people could do that.

Yep, it had been fun. I'd been buzzing. Until now.

"She was here, wasn't she?" I asked.

Jess didn't answer. She didn't need to.

This particular incident wasn't someone sending me bullet cartridges or coming at me with a knife but it told me something.

My stalker was getting closer.

Whereas the only person I wanted to get closer to was Jess.

CHAPTER TWELVE

Jess

Lachie hadn't been kidding when he'd said he wanted to visit my aunt and uncle. I was going along with it even though it seemed a little odd. Besides, my aunt would never forgive me if she found out Lachie Tyler had wanted to stop by her house and I hadn't let him. Better not to go there.

The gig at Charlie's a few days ago had been more of a risk than I'd realized. Andrew knew the store and surroundings, and had assured me we'd have good access and control. Even though we'd had no chance for much in the way of planning, it could've been a lot worse.

One thing I knew for sure. If someone was going to attack, it would happen quickly. It'd be over in seconds. Lachie thought I was overreacting. I wasn't.

Aunt Rachel's was a much safer bet. I didn't have to worry about concealed places where an attacker might be hidden or manning the boundaries. Walking through her front door made the rest of the world seem so far away.

It wasn't just the smell of baking or seeing the familiar living room with the comfy sofa and the Oregon coffee table Uncle Mark had made. It was the feeling of coming home that filled me with warmth.

Aunt Rachel hadn't stopped smiling since we'd walked in the door. Hadn't stopped talking either. Lachie and I were sitting on her sofa while she sat on an armchair opposite us, all the better to stare and admire him.

She gestured to the spread she'd laid out on the coffee table, her eyes still on Lachie. "I hope you like cupcakes."

"I *love* cupcakes." He placed one on a plate and took a bite. "Delicious."

"What about me?" I didn't care if I sounded petulant. I was her niece, not him, and I'd always been her favorite, something that had made all the difference through my teenage years. She'd made me feel loved and I'd never forget it.

"The pink icing is for you, darling," she said. "I know how you like it."

"I do, thanks." Now that the natural order had been restored, I felt warmed on the inside again. "Such a shame Uncle Mark couldn't be here."

He was a plumber and worked for himself so he couldn't afford to turn down clients and take the day off. Aunt Rachel worked part-time as a teacher so we'd made sure to come on her day off.

"Well, then, you'll have to come over again," she said.

"Sure we can." Lachie jumped in before I could say anything.

"What's it like being a famous rock star?" she asked, then seeing the expression on my face added, "Don't look at me like that."

Lachie spread his arms. "I'm a guy who plays in a band. I don't really think of myself that way."

"So do you have female fans chasing after you all the time? Is it a different girl every night?"

"Aunt Rachel!" I bit back my anxiety. There hadn't been any other women at Lachie's place, not so far, and I wasn't sure if it meant anything.

He took it in his stride. "Uh, it's not like the Playboy Mansion. I have a very nice place, one of the perks of the job, but it's not a palace or anything. And it's certainly not a never ending parade of women."

"What about everything else that goes with it? Taking drugs, trashing hotels, getting arrested?"

I brought a hand to my temple. Sometimes my aunt just wouldn't give up.

He laughed it off. "None of the above."

Not lately anyway. At a guess, I'd say he'd done some drugs in the past and I'd heard about him and Nick trashing the band room at The Swamp, which seemed especially ludicrous since Nick owned the place.

My aunt was on a roll. "Jess told me you had a stalker and that's why she's with you. She didn't say much else."

I swallowed the last mouthful of cupcake. "You know I can't get into details."

"It's okay, Jess." Lachie looked across at my aunt. "Most of our fans are fabulous. That's kind of why we do this. In the hope people will like our music and buy our records. But now there's this weirdo woman—we think it's a woman—who has crossed the line. It started off with some Facebook messages that were freaky but didn't seem like anything to worry about. Would've been fine if she'd stopped there."

Lachie seemed to be on his best behavior and maybe I should be grateful. Instead, I heard the trepidation in his voice, saw the anxiety in his features, and wished I could make all of that go away.

Aunt Rachel raised her eyebrows. "So you haven't been attacked or anything?"

"No, I haven't."

Not yet. And it was my job to make sure it stayed that way.

The police had been remarkably quick with their forensic testing so we already had Lachie's car back. I had to wonder if his vehicle received priority because he was famous. It might be one of the perks of fame but ironically it was fame that had got him into this situation.

The police believed they had some good fingerprints from the car, several sets in fact, because the stalker wasn't the only person who'd touched Lachie's SUV. So far, none of the prints matched any known offenders, which told us Lachie's stalker hadn't committed any crimes before or hadn't been caught. If there'd been a match, this would've been so much easier.

Also, as weird as it sounded, the authorities had sent the feces off for analysis because there would be DNA in the cells of human tissue.

Aunt Rachel nodded. "As long as you're staying safe. Taking care of yourself."

Lachie smiled. "That's kind of what Jess is for. Sometimes I forget she's a bodyguard, but that's what she is."

"And I hope you're taking care of Jess too."

Her voice was sharp enough to make Lachie sit upright.

He slipped his hand on my knee, his gaze riveted to my aunt's. "I'd love to help take care of her. Problem is,

I'm not sure she wants me to."

My mouth fell open, my eyes fixed ahead of me. I didn't dare look anywhere else either, didn't know what I wanted, except I did.

Longing surged inside, swelled in my chest, and yet there always seemed to be part of me that couldn't let go. I hated being so controlled, despised that side of myself, and couldn't work out why this should be so hard. I only knew that it was.

Lachie slid his hand away, the place where his fingers had been suddenly cool. I missed his touch almost immediately.

Aunt Rachel hadn't finished yet. "I never approved of Jess moving into security work. It seemed such a backward step." To me, "You were such a wonderful kindergarten teacher." Then to Lachie, "I'm not just saying that. It's true. I've spoken to the other teachers at school and a couple of the parents. She wasn't just good. The kids loved her and learned from her. And I think she loved it too."

A pang cut through my heart at the memory of a roomful of five-year-olds looking up at me expectantly. My aunt was right. I'd loved that job and loved the kids too. Maybe I'd still be there if I hadn't lost my job, but there was another side of me and other things I loved as well.

Lachie turned to me. "I can't picture you working with little kids. It's almost as if you're two people, a bit like a split personality, because the Jess I know is a different person. Is it because your aunt is a teacher? Is that what inspired you to take it up too?"

"Kind of," I said. "Aunt Rachel is a natural in the role."

She lowered her gaze. "No, I'm not happy about Jess

being a bodyguard, but what can you do? She has to live her own life and make her own choices. It's hard to let go and that's what we've had to do."

"It's what all parents have to do eventually." Lachie froze as soon as the words came out of his mouth, realizing these weren't my parents.

But my aunt was unstoppable. "We're so lucky to have Jess. It couldn't have worked out better for us. We always wanted children. Couldn't have them. I was cut up about it for years." Her face clouding over, she held a hand out. "But that's another story. Then Jess moved to Frankston with her parents, which was wonderful and then she came to live with us and it was as if she'd always been a part of our family. Well, she was a part of our family, obviously. And she's so much more because we *chose* her and that makes her special. We loved her right from the start."

Aunt Rachel was beaming in a way my own mom never had, glowing from a place deep within, her face expressing everything she felt inside.

I took a deep breath to stop the tears burning at the back of my eyes. It felt good to be loved, wanted, cared for, even if Aunt Rachel wasn't my mom.

"I'm so glad your parents moved to Frankston." Her eyes glittered, her face serene. "I can't imagine all those years without you."

"How old were you when your folks moved here?" Lachie asked me.

"Fourteen," I said.

"A trying time," Aunt Rachel added. "That horrible incident happened only a few months after that. Still, she has blossomed since then."

My face reddened, nerves coursing through me. *Change*

the subject. Think of something.

Aunt Rachel kept talking. "And two years later, Cathie and David, that's Jess's parents, moved to California to follow their dream. Cathie was always like that, flighty, a free spirit. I tried to talk her out of it but, for whatever reason, she thought it was for the best. It worked out beautifully for me and Mark, though. We loved having Jess with us."

Suddenly I was thankful for my aunt's incessant chatter. Relieved. Because we'd moved on.

Lachie turned to me, raised his eyebrows. "So your parents moved to California and … you stayed here?"

He was being tactful. They left me behind. That was what had happened.

"Yes." Time to change the subject once and for all, so I turned to my aunt. "Didn't you have some CDs you wanted Lachie to autograph?"

She got up and grabbed a couple of CDs and a black marker that were conveniently waiting on the TV cabinet behind her. Lachie took them from her, pulled the covers out from beneath the plastic, and signed them.

Aunt Rachel sat back down. "Imagine, if the only place I had my music was on my phone, I wouldn't be able to get Lachie to autograph these for me. I'm not a big fan of downloading and iTunes and live streaming."

"Live streaming is for TV shows," I said.

She waved it off. "Whatever. I've downloaded CDs onto the iPod on my phone. I'm not completely out of touch. It was so different in my day, much more exciting, I think. We'd save up to buy records. They've got such beautiful big covers, not like these tiny CDs."

"People are buying records again," I said. "Vinyl is hot.

Highly desirable."

"Really? Just as well I've still got my old records then."

I got up and kissed my aunt on the cheek. "Probably time for us to go."

She stayed seated, took my hand into hers. "You'll be careful, won't you?" Then to Lachie. "I'm depending on you."

"Okay, yep, for sure." For a moment, Lachie looked like a school kid being sent to the principal's office.

Aunt Rachel put the cups and plates onto the tray she'd left on the coffee table. Lachie swept it from the table and stood.

"Oh, I can do that," my aunt said.

"It's no problem at all." He strode to the kitchen, returning in a flash.

Aunt Rachel kept talking as she walked us to the door, saying how she never thought she'd have a real live rock star in her house. Remarkably, being star struck didn't stop her from being a chatterbox. Not that I minded. It was one of the things that made me feel at home here.

At the door, I switched into a different mode. I always kept my eyes out on our way to the car and as we were getting in and out. Lachie might think it was overkill but I didn't.

When we were well on our way, I said, "So what was with sucking up to my aunt?"

"Me?" Indignation in his voice.

"Yeah, you were so well behaved, so polite, taking the coffee cups back to the kitchen. That didn't seem like your style."

"What are you talking about? I wasn't sucking up. I was scared of her."

We both laughed.

After a while he asked, "What happened when you were fourteen, Jess?"

I gritted my teeth. "What do you mean?"

"Your aunt mentioned a horrible incident."

Flicking on my indicator, I put my foot down and overtook the car in front. "I need to concentrate on driving, sorry."

Lachie had asked the one question I didn't want to answer. He was kind and didn't press the point. Meanwhile the memories kept coming back to me, my gut tightening as I forced myself to concentrate on the traffic and our route.

Damn it, I wasn't fourteen anymore. I didn't need to go there. Yet I couldn't get it off my mind, the events playing on a loop in my head, those old feelings coming back to me.

When we reached Lachie's house and I locked the front door behind us, he looked at me as if expecting something. I expected more of myself too.

"I don't normally talk about it," I said. Understatement of the year.

He stopped in the hallway, gave me some space.

And I had to get if off my chest. "I wasn't like you as a teenager. When we came here, I was the new kid at school, and I didn't fit in. My clothes weren't right. Nothing about me was right. I was looking for a small group of friends like I used to have at my old school and I couldn't find them."

"Everyone needs friends."

"Well, I didn't have any. I wasn't exactly being bullied at school or anything. It was more that it hurt to be excluded all the time. It felt as if everyone else was having a big party and I wasn't invited. I don't even know why it happened."

"Why what happened?"

"It was a Saturday. I was on the bus on my way to the mall. Mom had given me money to buy a new pair of jeans and I was hoping to bump into some girls from school while I was there. I didn't make it that far."

He nodded for me to continue.

"Some older girls from my school got on the bus. I'd seen them around. They were so loud it was hard to miss them. One of them, Olivia, came up and started shoving me in the shoulder, demanding my purse. I wouldn't give it to her. I shook my head, barely said a word. Then she pulled me off the seat and started hitting me. Hard. Proper punches, not little girly slaps. I ended up on the floor in the aisle and she kept kicking me while I was down."

He placed his hands on my shoulders. "Were there other people on the bus? Did anyone try to stop her?"

"That's the thing." My voice cracked. "No one did anything. Not a thing. No one even called out to the driver. The girls moved to the back of the bus, laughing, while I lay there moaning in pain. And an old lady shushed me, told me to get up and stop whimpering. That was what really killed me, sucked the air right out of me. As if I was the one making trouble."

"Oh, Jess."

"I forced myself to get up. There were a couple of people standing in the aisle ahead of me. Maybe the driver couldn't see what was going on, I don't know. I dragged myself off the bus and walked all the way back home."

My throat tight, I swallowed back the pain. I hadn't

forgotten the bruised ribs that made it hard for me to breathe, the black eye, the gash on my head that bled all over my clothes. I hadn't forgotten any of it.

But the true torture was in all those people who'd done nothing, who'd watched and hadn't cared. All those people and no one had done anything. I still couldn't get it through my head. And sometimes I couldn't get the hurt out of my heart either.

For months, I had flashbacks. I'd see the old lady, the scorn in her face, the scowl that told me I was nothing. And it was as if I was back on that bus being hit and kicked on the ground.

For weeks, I hadn't been able to get out of bed and had dreaded going back to school. Eventually I did, and life went back to normal. On the outside.

Lachie pulled me close, strong arms wrapped around me. My head resting on his chest, I breathed in his manly smell, the citrus from his shampoo, traces of something that could only be Lachie.

A strange feeling flooded through me, as if I belonged, as if this was meant to be, and maybe the world wasn't so bad after all. Perhaps in talking about the attack, I was giving him a piece of myself.

"I can't imagine anyone wanting to hurt you like that," he whispered.

And I still didn't even know why. I hadn't done anything and only knew those girls by sight. Olivia had picked on me because she knew I was a victim, that was the only part I was sure about. My breath caught in my throat.

"What happened to those girls?" he asked.

Gathering my strength, I pulled away. "Olivia got

charged with something and had to do community service. She blamed me. Told me it was my fault."

"Man, she must be a piece of work." He held me at arm's length. "I take it you weren't a kickboxer back then."

Tears burning at the back of my eyes, I sucked in a deep breath to hold them back. Aunt Rachel was the one who'd suggested martial arts to get me out of the hole I was in, though she'd since forgotten that part, and Mom was the one who took me to my first lesson. My world changed. For the better.

I twisted my hands. "At least one good thing came out of that horrible day."

I was strong now, faster, better able to take care of myself, not scared anymore. I'd found my place in the world. Everyone needed to belong and I wasn't any different.

Lachie cupped my chin in his hands, the air between us charged. My heart stood still because I knew what was coming as he pressed his lips against mine. The kiss was gentle, chaste, everything I wanted and not what I wanted at all.

Gazing into my eyes, he gave me a moment, then pulled me closer. I tilted my head, sliding my arms behind his neck and we kissed, bodies pressed up close, tongues rolling, emotions surging. I ran my hands through his hair.

He pushed me up against the wall in the hallway, ran his hands over my hips, my waist, my breasts. I reached for his butt and pulled him close, throwing us into another kiss.

Fear and uncertainty mixed with the desire spreading through my body. I wanted this. And I didn't. I couldn't let this happen.

Eventually, I edged away. "I have to check the house."

I walked away. I didn't have to check the house, not when it was locked when we'd walked in. How pathetic was that? How pathetic was I?

I shouldn't be getting all flustered over something as simple as a kiss. I was a grown woman. I'd dated other guys, been in relationships. It wasn't as though this was my first time.

Except, damn it, I shouldn't be kissing him at all. I was supposed to be the bodyguard, alert, aware, anticipating. And the thing I was anticipating wasn't meant to be sex. This was all wrong.

I couldn't work it out. Sometimes I was a scared little girl again and sometimes I was a hard ass.

Maybe that was part of the problem. I was so used to taking care of myself that I found it hard to let go and let anyone else in.

CHAPTER THIRTEEN

Lachie

Not so long ago, Nick and I would've been going out, finding the grungiest bars and drinking till we couldn't stand up. Sometimes longer. Now here we were, gathered around the table on my back patio and there was nowhere I'd rather be.

I still liked to have a drink but didn't want to keep going the way I had been. Besides, I couldn't get drunk enough to block out the pain from my father being so ill. I'd tried that enough times and it hadn't helped.

There was something else too. I was staying sober because being drunk was no way to get into a relationship. You'd think I'd have learned that much by now.

Nick and Lily had dropped by and stayed for a barbecue dinner, so it felt almost like two old married couples getting together, except for the fact that Nick and Lily weren't married yet, and Jess and I were locked in some weird holding pattern.

Four-year-old Thomas had been sitting at table with us, "like a grown up" in his words, before scampering onto the grass where he was throwing a ball up in the air. We all heard a splash and turned.

"Uh-oh." He stood there, a guilty expression on his face.

Through the glass pool fencing, we could all see his red and yellow ball floating near the edge of the pool. It looked almost as guilty as he did.

"You didn't throw the ball over there on purpose, did you?" Nick asked.

Thomas shook his head. "No, Daddy."

"It's okay, dude, but maybe you can try to be a bit more careful."

So strange seeing Nick in father-mode, something else I should be used to by now but clearly I hadn't paid much attention before.

Nick had his hands on the arm of his chair ready to get up, when Jess stood first. "I'll get it."

"Hey, Thomas." She wandered closer to him. "I'll grab the ball and throw it over for you to catch."

"I'm not a very good catch." He brightened. "It's my ball. *I* should be the one to get it."

Lily's head jerked as she grabbed Nick's hand, clearly unhappy about something.

Jess crouched down to his height. "You can only go inside the pool enclosure if you hold my hand the whole time." She looked across at Nick and Lily. "Is that okay?"

Lily let go of Nick. "Sure."

What was going on? Maybe she had a problem with kids being around water. Thomas had had an accident in the bath so maybe that was what this was all about.

All stuff I would never have noticed before. It was amazing the bits and pieces I was picking up now since I'd only had one beer. That counted as sober.

Jess was in her element holding Thomas's hand as she lifted the child-proof lock and let him into the pool enclosure, chatting to him the whole time.

He pointed with his free hand. "You've got a hot tub."

"Yeah, that's right."

"I'd love to go in the hot tub." His high-pitched voice sailed through the evening air.

"Maybe another time, and we'd have to check with your parents. Now you stand there while I get the ball." She leaned over, reached into the pool for the ball, and passed it to him. "Do you want to bounce it to get the water off?"

He did exactly that. Jess made a big deal out of pretending to be wet, which caused all sorts of hilarity with Thomas. The kid just loved to giggle. Then she took his hand and led him back into the yard where he followed her to the table, clambering up onto his chair between hers and Lily's.

"Can I have some more sausage, Mommy?"

"Sure, honey. You don't mind that it'll be cold?"

"It'll be yummy."

Lily stabbed one end of a sausage with a fork and passed it over to him so he could grab the fork handle. He nibbled from the top, then made the sausage sway on the fork and started singing a little song. This wasn't just food. It was entertainment.

Something made me think it wouldn't be too terrible to have kids, one day, far, far into the future.

"Hey," Nick said. "That guy Domino has been in touch."

I shrugged. "Who?"

"Bass player. I told you about him."

"Oh, yeah."

"I've had a lot on my mind, what with the wedding plans and all, but we should get together with him, see what he's like."

"Yeah, we should." And I should muster up some enthusiasm. "It's just such a drag. Feels like we're starting all over again."

"What are you talking about? This is nothing like starting from scratch." Nick tilted his head, stared. "You're not still pissed at Austin, are you?"

Not much I wasn't. Still, I didn't want to get into this now and Nick didn't get it anyway, couldn't understand why I felt so let down, why Austin's timing was so bad. The Merchants of Menace was a band—our band, a part of us—and a bass player wasn't something you could replace like changing a wheel on car.

"Austin is ancient history." I opened a second beer. Two beers wasn't exactly going overboard.

"You should get together with him again, dude. Soon. I'm telling you, he's got his sh—" Nick glanced at Thomas, "—his act together. He's a seriously good architect and has some great ideas when it comes to renovating the bar. Things are working out for him. He and Tara seem happy together."

"Daddy, you didn't tell them about how I'm going to carry the ring."

Thomas seemed to come out with whatever entered his head and, in this case, I didn't mind one little bit.

"It's a very important job," he said loudly in case we hadn't heard the first time.

Lily leaned across and gave him a hug. "That's true."

"Ooh, so what do you have to do exactly?" Jess

sounded super enthusiastic, the way people did when they talked to kids.

"The ring will be on a cushion." He put the sausage back on his plate. "And I have to carry the cushion down the aisle all by myself. Daddy will be at the front and then Auntie Scarlett and Mommy will come behind me. I'll be leading the team."

Jess smiled. "Yep, that sounds like leadership material."

Thomas told us a bit more about his very important duties, then said he was going to play with his yellow truck. Two minutes later, he was making vroom vroom sounds and chatting to himself.

"We'll have to get going soon." Lily looked at Nick. "It's past his bedtime."

"Sure, honey." Nick shifted his gaze to Lachie. "You haven't said anything about your car and how all that turned out."

I sighed. "Jess can fill you in."

She let them know about the police investigation, fingerprints and forensic testing while I sat there drinking my beer while trying not to look fed up.

"You know the old saying?" Nick said. "You can't dust for poop."

I screwed up my face. "Huh?"

He spread his hands. "It's a joke. Like the line in *Spinal Tap* where the guy says you can't dust for vomit."

I laughed, couldn't help myself when it came to the occasional bit of gross-out humor. The scene about the fictional singer who'd supposedly choked on his own vomit was still funny.

Jess smiled and Lily was shaking her head.

"Actually," Jess said. "Forensics has come a long way since that movie. There's DNA in poop, which is why they can test for it."

Lily squirmed. "The whole thing is pretty revolting."

Jess nodded. "Yeah, it is."

Thomas ran up to the table. "Are you guys talking about *poop*?"

Lily pushed her chair back. "Our cue to leave."

"Tell me about the poop, Mommy." Thomas tugged at her arm.

She asked him to collect his toys, doing the distraction-thing that parents seemed to be so good at. This was a different world. Not a bad world. In fact, at the moment Nick and Lily seemed to be in a better place than I was.

I had Jess in my life and I didn't, which wasn't nearly good enough because I wanted her to hang around and be part of my life, for a while anyway.

She helped me clean up and bring in the dirty plates from the patio, not because I asked but because she always helped out. After a final look around, she locked the back door and joined me in the kitchen.

This was her version of being at ease. At least she was more relaxed than when we went out somewhere.

"You never talk about Austin." She leaned against the counter. "Whereas you talk about Nick and Cooper and even your manager and the recording guy."

There'd been a time when I'd have left the tidying up for someone else. I had a housekeeper, after all, but figured it wasn't beyond me to load the dishwasher.

I stacked the plates inside the machine. "There's a lot of things you don't talk about either."

"True."

I tried to pull the words together. "A band is like a family. Or it is when you've been together as long as we have. It wasn't always like that. Our first drummer was a an addict who sold one of Nick's guitars to buy smack, and our old bass player was a bit of a dick. Then, once we had Austin, we knew we were onto something. And we made it, but the problem with this industry is that you've never made it. There's always someone trying to screw you."

"So how is any of this Austin's fault?"

"He let us down. He's sure as hell let *me* down. We need him."

I couldn't explain why this was such a critical time, not without giving too much away, something I couldn't do because there was no way I could betray that particular confidence. Nick seemed to be over it, though, and Cooper had other things to worry about. Which only left me.

"Isn't he allowed to change his mind and decide on his own future?" Jess took my hands into hers. "Sorry if I sound pushy. I'm just asking."

Maybe I couldn't let go of the childish dream of the four of us guys hanging out forever. There was no 'maybe' about it. Jess was right.

More than that. She was right ... for me.

I stepped closer, invading her personal space, because that was what I wanted to do. Invade every inch of her.

"I'm done talking about Austin," I said.

She lifted her fingers to my lips, touching them lightly as she looked into my eyes. Her touch gentle, she slid her hand along my jawline, running her fingers through my hair at the back.

She wanted it. I wanted it.

I took her into my arms and kissed her, hard and hungry, because that's how I felt. I'd kissed her before and I'd let her go, a mistake I wasn't making again. I'd had my hands on her once before too.

And tonight I was going to have all of her.

She was pressed up against the counter, her back arched so I ravished her neck, scattering little kisses along the bare skin, then nuzzled closer. She smelled so good and she smelled of nothing. Just Jess.

And she felt so good. All woman. My hands were all over her, and hers all over me, as she ripped open the buttons on my shirt. I pulled up her T-shirt, my fingers on the bare skin of her waist, then higher, on those boobs I'd been dying to get my hands on.

I was hard, ready to take her there and then. God only knew I'd had sex in stupider places than the kitchen, in public places, anywhere I wanted. But I wanted to do this right. It had to be the bedroom.

Taking her hand into mine, I gazed into those soulful gray eyes and saw the teenager who'd been damaged, the girl who'd grown up, who needed to be protected as well. It sent a pang through my heart because I didn't want to see her hurt ever again.

I led her to the bedroom, her footsteps light behind me, though she probably wasn't the sort who followed men around.

Standing by the bed, she slid the shirt from my shoulders and kissed my neck and chest. Peppered a little circle of kisses around the new tattoo on my chest. So sweet. But she wasn't sweet and neither was I.

She fumbled with the button of my jeans, then gave up when I started shucking off the jeans myself. She ripped off her T-shirt, pants, and underwear.

Then she pushed me onto the bed. Blood roared through my veins, surging to one particular part of my body, sexual desire coursing through me like a rocket. She kissed and licked her way from my chest, going lower, driving me crazy. But no, I couldn't let it happen like this.

I rolled her over onto her side and whispered, "Not yet. Tonight, I'm going to take care of you."

Which is exactly what I did. I went down on her, taking pleasure in her fast breaths, her moans, the gentle squeal as she came.

Time meant nothing. We had all the time in the world, rolling around on the bed, making love, speaking to each other with our fingers, our mouths, our entire bodies. The strangest feeling overcame me, as if this was meant to be, as if we should stay this way for as long as we could.

Later, we were lying side by side, sated. For how long, I didn't know. A slight sense of desperation tugged away at me, a fear that this was too good to last, that she might somehow slip through my fingers. Where had that even come from?

I touched the tattoo on her hip. A tiny heart, so simple and so complex. "Do you believe in love, Jess?"

"Of course I do. I have to."

And there it was. *She had to.* A hint of melancholy that made me wonder if this was a heart or heartache.

"I didn't even know you had any tattoos," I said.

"I have another, on my ankle."

She sat up, showing me another small tattoo, this one of a pair of boxing gloves. Now that made perfect sense.

"I've never noticed it before," I said. "It's cute."

She wore jeans or pants because she was always on

duty and needed to wear something practical, so I'd never even seen her bare ankles, which seemed kind of strange now I thought about it.

Jess nudged me gently with her foot. "It's not cute. It's kick ass."

"Yep, that's exactly what I meant."

She stretched out those long legs, lean and toned from years of kickboxing. From here, I could admire the curve of her hips, the dip of her waist, and the outline of her abdominals in the dim light. It wasn't just that her stomach was flat. She had muscles. Everywhere.

I reached across, tickling her waist. I couldn't help myself. She giggled, something I wasn't sure I'd heard before, while my fingers gripped her taut stomach, the muscles rippling beneath.

"Man, they're some abs you've got."

She stopped laughing. "I hope you mean that in a good way."

"In the best way possible." I sat up to join her, my hands inching higher toward her boobs. I took them into my hands, unable to believe anyone could feel this good. "I like these muscles. They're so soft."

She laughed, a beautiful sound.

"I want you to stay here tonight," I said. "All night."

"You know I can't do that."

"You did it before."

"That was different. It was … an accident."

Why should she be so shy, so reluctant?

"And this is a deliberate decision." I nuzzled closer. "Because this is right, Jess. This is me and you. Besides, you need to be close to protect me."

She pressed her lips against mine, pushing me back

onto the bed, and I didn't resist. I took everything she threw my way.

This was exactly what I'd been waiting for and at the same time, it was more than I'd ever known I wanted. Jess was always looking out for me and not just because it was her job. No, that couldn't be the only reason.

I was finally seeing through that tough veneer, the part of herself that she showed the world, and it was all so clear to me now.

She was only hard on the outside.

Besides, this wasn't just sex. It was so much more. I wanted to protect her too and keep her safe because that was what you did when you truly cared for someone. When you loved them.

CHAPTER FOURTEEN

Jess

From bodyguard to lover and back again. What was I doing? How could I have let this happen? And how could I not?

I looked across the table at my hard ass, devil-may-care, guitar player boyfriend, and swallowed the lump in my throat. He wasn't my boyfriend. I didn't know what he was, only that I'd fallen way too hard. And now that we were in a public place, I couldn't let myself be distracted.

Glancing around The Swamp, I took in the lunchtime crowd, people chatting and eating at their tables, some sitting on stools at the bar, and one of Andrew's guys looking out across the room, his half-drunk glass of water on the bar behind him.

At least I'd been fed, and very nicely too. Lachie had arranged to meet Austin, insisting the two of us should have lunch first because his ex-bass player couldn't make it until a little later. Lachie had devoured a giant steak while I'd had grilled chicken and salad, thereby combining protein and nutrients because when I was on the job, I always made sure I ate healthily.

A waitress cleared our table. I'd already noticed that Tara, the bar manager, wasn't here today.

"We've got some time before Austin gets here." I handed Lachie my phone. "Maybe you can take another look at the footage."

He pursed his lips. "Okay, then."

It was just as well I'd spoken to the two teenage boys, Joey and Oliver, when Lachie and Nick had done their impromptu set at Charlie's. That had made it easy to get in touch with them. It was lucky also that they were 'documenting' the performance because they'd shot plenty of footage of the crowd. The boys had been very obliging in sharing the video they'd taken too. I hadn't even needed to tell them about the stalker or Lachie's car. The kids were just happy to help.

I'd sent the footage to Andrew who had forwarded it to the police. If anything came of this, it might add up to evidence of some sort, but that was the problem. We didn't know who the stalker was, so we could only react and couldn't do anything until she did something first.

"Anything?" I asked.

Lachie shrugged. "There's no one I've seen before, nothing that seems weird, no one who looks suspicious."

At least he'd looked at the footage properly now. When I'd first shown him, he'd been blinded by anger and unable to take it all in.

He nudged my phone closer to me. "It's just a bunch of people watching us play. I mean, can *you* see anything jumping out at you?"

I shook my head. I'd examined the footage over and over, so many times it was committed to memory. I'd looked at the faces and expressions. All fans. Or at the very least, people who were enjoying themselves so nothing stood out as remarkable or unusual.

Quite a crowd had gathered by the time Lachie and Nick had finished playing. Parents with kids, guitar players and musicians, their friends, several groups of girls, a young woman with lots of brown hair covering her face, people who'd come down from the CD store, others too. A mixed crowd.

Nothing and no one had stood out as strange that day, even though I'd been ready to act if necessary. I knew how things were likely to go down. If an attacker was present, there'd be a moment of recognition, only a moment. Then I'd have to cover Lachie, stop the attack, subdue the attacker, and get Lachie the hell out of there.

It was always better to be close to an attacker, critical in fact, because that closeness was key. Otherwise that person would have more chance of success. The last thing we wanted.

"Lachie, I didn't see anything weird that day," I said. "If I had, I'd have taken action."

But his stalker had been there, had left a little present in his car for him, and we were none the wiser. He didn't need to be reminded of this.

"I'm going to the bathroom." He pushed his chair back, then motioned toward the bar. "I've seen him before. That's one of Andrew's guys, isn't it?"

"Yes."

"He's going to follow me to the men's, isn't he?"

"Yes."

Lachie grimaced. "There's no such thing as a nice quiet lunch, the two of us."

Unfortunately, there wasn't. I felt for him, truly I did. I

also had a job to do.

I watched him leave and the security guard follow. Later, movement in the doorway caught my eye as Austin walked into the bar. He was hard to miss with his quiff, pointy sideburns and bowling shirt.

He didn't know me but I got up and greeted him anyway. "I'm Jess, a friend of Lachie's."

"Nice to meet you." He shook my hand. "Is Lachie around?"

I pointed behind him. "He's coming now."

Lachie had a smile in his eyes as he strode up, then shook his hand. "Man, you've got to get a move on with the renovations and bring this place up to scratch."

He'd already told me Austin was Nick's architect for the bar's restoration.

Austin nodded. "I'm working on it."

"It's funny. The bathrooms have been cleaned up but there's still some guy in there who's so drunk he can't piss straight." Lachie shook his head, his expression part way between embarrassed and annoyed. "Like the old days. I remember starting a fight with someone over that once before."

"Fond memories, eh?"

He waved it off. "Forget about that. It's on to more serious matters. I'm offended."

Austin raised his eyebrows. "Sorry?"

"You didn't use me as a design consultant. Surely you would've needed input from an expert in drunkenness, debauchery, and dive bars. Someone like me." He spread his arms. "Aren't I exactly the sort of clientele you want to attract to a place like this?"

Austin laughed and if I'd had any doubts, I didn't now.

The two of them were going to get on just fine. Lachie would make sure of it.

Austin explained he didn't have much time because a client had called a meeting at the last minute, but that he hadn't wanted to cancel on Lachie. I kept my distance while the two of them sat down and talked—a safe distance, which meant I stayed close.

After a while, Austin got up and left, waving goodbye to me.

Lachie joined me. "You were right about talking to him. I got a few things off my chest."

It must've taken a lot for him to say that, a guy like Lachie who was probably used to people pandering to him. He'd had to take a step back and look at things afresh.

Lachie looked content, something that was good to see. "I told him it was okay that he'd wanted to leave The Merchants, that he was getting back into architecture and doing what he wanted. It was just two old friends getting together for a bit and I told him we'd catch up properly another time, the four of us."

"The four of us?"

"Yeah, the two of us with him and Tara. She's into rockabilly too."

I nodded. "I've met her."

"Austin's got a new band together, a rockabilly outfit. It's strange. There was a bit of a pang when he told me that, but I'm pleased for him. He's got his thing and I've got mine."

And I had Lachie. Or I hoped I did. I longed for there to be a 'two of us' just as he'd said. I liked the way those words had rolled off his tongue as if it was the most natural thing in the world.

And now I had to make sure we got back home safely. I called the other security guy over and he walked with us to the car. The drive back to Lachie's was uneventful, just the way I liked it. He didn't say much and I didn't mind because I could concentrate on driving. I was aware he sometimes thought my precautions were overkill but I couldn't let that bother me or affect my decision-making.

Fifteen minutes later, we were back at his place. Lachie wandered through the house to the back door where he stepped outside onto the patio. We were in the shade, sheltered from the sun that glittered on the smooth surface of the pool. Still, the sun had a bite to it. That was Nevada for you.

His eyes glued to the pool, he intertwined his fingers around mine. "Looks inviting, doesn't it?"

"Sure does."

He turned to me. "I don't want a swim. I want you."

I smiled, couldn't help myself. "Well, you're in luck. Because that can be arranged."

He slid his hand onto my waist, nuzzling into my neck. It sent a sizzle up my spine and, if I was a different person in another situation, I would have kept going with this right here and now, outside, in the open. We could have taken our clothes off and jumped into the pool or the hot tub. We could have never gotten out of the hot tub, for that matter.

But it was safer inside, so I led him back into the house. Lachie's gaze was on my hand as I locked the door behind us, his expression bordering on a scowl. I didn't like this anymore than he did, but this was the most basic of security measures and not something I could ignore.

I stepped forward and cupped his face in my hands. *I love you.* The words were on the tip of my tongue. Why would I even think of coming out with that now in the middle of a perfectly ordinary moment?

Not that I'd ever say it. I couldn't. Lachie had been with lots of girls and there was no reason for me to think I was special, no reason he should love me back.

He covered my mouth with his, stopped me from thinking, and kissed me in a way that made me forget everything else. Because sometimes I wanted to forget. I wanted to be loved. Was that so bad?

Suddenly I felt a strange vibration between us and for a moment, couldn't work out what was going on. Then Lachie pulled his phone out of his jeans pocket. It was on silent but must've been set to vibrate.

I sniggered, covering my mouth. "And I thought *I'd* done that to you!"

Lachie smiled, albeit reluctantly, as he glanced at his phone. "It's Nick." He shook his head. "Sorry, I shouldn't even have looked."

"No, it's okay. You should take it."

Lachie put the phone to his ear.

The moment had been lost and there'd be other moments, if what he'd said at the bar was anything to go by. Besides, it wouldn't take long to get back in the mood when I was with him.

"When?" Lachie raked a hand through his hair, his shoulders slumped as he turned away. "Who else? Are you sure?"

I stepped around and placed a hand on his shoulder. The color had drained from his face, his green eyes glazed. Whatever was going on, it wasn't good.

Dropping his hand, he pressed the phone off. "Nick received an invitation from my stalker."

"Yeah?"

"To my wedding."

My gut clenched. His stalker was so deluded she believed the two of them were getting married. One minute she was threatening to shoot him and sending him bullet cartridges, and now this. It didn't make sense and that made this all the more complex because this person was unhinged and unpredictable.

"Cooper got one too. Not Austin, though. Nick phoned around first." Lachie's voice faltered. "He's sent a picture of the invitation."

Lachie looked down at his phone, then stepped closer to show me.

The words at the top were in a large cursive font—The Greatest Love of My Life—followed by an invitation from Lachie Tyler to celebrate his forthcoming union to his Angel as ordained by god above, along with the date, time, and venue.

No wonder Lachie was freaked.

CHAPTER FIFTEEN

Lachie

It had been weird having a bodyguard at first. I'd felt like a kid who needed adult supervision or a prisoner being escorted to court, all of which was about as far from warm and fuzzy as you could get. Not to mention which, I wasn't used to any of it.

We'd moved on since then. Jess was still the bodyguard. Too many things happened every day to remind me of that, only whereas before I'd been resentful, now I liked having her around. A lot.

I didn't need an excuse to call her. She was just there. Which was strange too, because in the past I'd had girls who wanted to hang around too long and I'd had to ask them to leave. I'd always hated it when things got to that stage. It felt so seedy.

And now the two of us were visiting my parents. Another strange thing. I hadn't brought a girl to meet my parents since high school or at least not since we'd started touring and the band had started getting big.

Dad was back at home and doing better, even if 'better' was a relative term. He was sitting in his favorite chair, which should've been fine except he couldn't even get up out of the chair on his own.

A grown man. Not that long ago, he'd been landscaping the backyard and repainting the house. He was always happier when he had a project on his hands. Now his only job was Project Getting Better.

Seeing him like this was killing me. I clenched my jaw, then forced myself to relax because I couldn't let my feelings show when it'd only make him feel worse.

Mom shot me a pointed look. "Lachie, can you please give me a hand in the kitchen?"

"You're never too old to help your mother," Dad instructed, then turned to Jess. "He's generally pretty good at helping around the home."

"Oh, he's very well house trained." She smiled, following us into the kitchen.

Mom dug something out of a drawer and said in a low voice. "I wanted to show you this."

Gold lettering on a cream card. A wedding invitation.

My gut clenched, nerve endings skittering. I'd seen the photo Nick sent me but somehow it was different seeing the invitation in the flesh. Salt into the wound.

"I didn't want your dad to see," Mom added. "He's got enough on his plate as it is."

Exactly what I'd been thinking minutes ago. "So do you."

The stalker knew where my parents lived. Anger bubbled inside me. She should stay the fuck away from them or I'd kill that bitch myself. This was too close, too personal.

I was reaching for the invitation when Jess held her hand out. "It's evidence. We'll show it to the police."

She asked Mom for a plastic bag, then slid the invitation inside, and placed it into the purse that was still slung over her shoulder. We hadn't even been here long enough for Jess to take her purse off. And now this.

I gritted my teeth, told myself the invitation was old news, nothing to get worked up about all over again. It didn't stop the blood from pounding in my temples.

"I'm sorry, Mom. Like Jess said, the police are onto this."

She placed her hand over mine. "I'm worried, darling."

"Look." I forced myself to sound reassuring. "For the first time in my life, I'm a lot more aware of what's going on around me. I've got a bodyguard, a team of bodyguards whenever I need them. This is just one weirdo and we've got it under control."

"Okay." Mom nodded, didn't look convinced.

"In the meantime, I think Dad needs a coffee."

Mom made coffee and a peppermint tea for Jess. I'd noticed she didn't have much caffeine when she was working, which was all the time. She took the tray Mom passed to her and went ahead of us.

"Jess seems like a good person." Mom leaned in close. "Dad and I both like her a lot."

I didn't know what to say since I wasn't exactly sure where I stood. "It's complicated."

"Life is always complicated. Your job is to work out what's best and keep things as simple as they can be."

Good old Mom always had to have the last word. And maybe she was right. Complications weren't something to be used as an excuse. They were just things to get through or get over. The hard part was knowing what you wanted, and if you had that straight, then everything else should follow.

In the living room, Jess passed my dad his coffee. He hadn't moved. No surprises there.

My eyes on Jess, I saw her in a new light. She'd been beaten, literally, when she was only a kid, yet she hadn't let that get in her way. She'd used it to grow into a stronger, more superior person.

I could use a little of that inner strength myself. And maybe somehow this experience with the stalker would shape me into a better person.

But I didn't want to be a better person. I wanted the stalker out of my life and Jess in it. I wanted to make love to her, see her naked, the fit body, the lean legs, toned arms, those amazing abs, so soft and hard and supple all at the same time. The blood rushed through my body all over again, this time for very different reasons.

Jess wandered to the mantel while Mom and I sat down, then pointed to a picture of me as a toddler. "You were so cute."

I raised my eyebrows. "Hey, I'm still cute."

Mom and Dad told a few obligatory stories from when I was growing up—about how obsessed I'd been with my tricycle as a kid, then my bike, then sports, and how I was always getting into trouble at school.

A slight exaggeration. It was just that I'd rather have been hanging with friends or playing my guitar than doing math. And no one could have predicted how successful and lucrative the band would turn out to be.

Mom and Dad had been there all the way. They'd paid for guitar lessons when I was a teenager and had come to plenty of gigs, some good, some bad. Some truly abysmal, if I was going to be honest. They'd never told me to give up on my dream or find a different ambition or get a 'real' job. They'd believed in me.

And now this. I looked at Dad stuck in his chair. My chest tightened, my throat too. He deserved a hell of a lot better than he was getting. If only he had something to look forward to the way I did.

"Nick and I have a radio performance coming up," I said. "Should be fun."

"When is that?" Dad asked.

"A few more days."

"When? What time?" His face lit up. "I'll have to listen in."

So I told him. Jess thought the event would be too dangerous, whereas I didn't.

I also didn't dare look at her. Maybe it was sneaky of me to bring this up now in front of my father when I knew she wouldn't say anything. Or couldn't. She was way too respectful for that.

Dad leaned forward to put his empty cup on the coffee table, something that took all his effort. "So how does that work?"

"It's a live interview on air where we perform a few songs in the studio. Then they want us to play a couple more songs in the square outside, and sign posters and CDs, that sort of thing."

That was the part Jess didn't approve of. The outdoor gig and public gathering.

My shoulders stiffening, I tried to shake it off. Jess and I had already clashed over this subject. Big-time.

I put the empty cups on the tray on the coffee table, motioning to Mom that I'd take care of this. When Jess followed, I knew what was coming and started bristling before she'd even said a word.

"Did you really have to bring that up, then?" she asked in a low voice.

"Why not?"

"Because you have to be careful. The situation is more complex than you think."

What had my mom said earlier? That you should try to keep things simple. Well, the simple fact of the matter was that I was a guitar player. I *liked* playing guitar. I lived for it. And fans expected the occasional public appearance. We wouldn't have gotten anywhere if not for the people who came to our gigs and bought our records. I couldn't forget that or I'd end up like some arrogant, spoilt, shitty, little rock star. I'd met enough of those along the way.

Jess held a hand out. "We can't talk about this now."

"Yeah, I could've told you that."

I stomped back into the living room, barely looked at her. Anger burning in my stomach, I hid it from my parents as we said goodbye, but I wasn't exactly hiding it from Jess as we drove back to my place. We couldn't even have an argument like two normal people, not in the car, not when Jess was set on concentrating on driving and her surroundings. It got my goat up even more.

I was still festering as we got out of the car, but I knew better than to say anything until we were inside the house. I'd been drilled too well about the risks of attack when getting in and out of the vehicle. Another thing that rankled.

As soon as she closed the front door behind us, I let rip. "It's a radio show. I don't see what the big deal is."

"The station has already been promoting it," she said. "That's part of the problem because everyone will know when you'll be there. If your stalker is planning something, that'll make things way too easy for her. It's giving her your location on a plate."

"She already knows where I live."

"That's different. Your house is a private, contained area." Jess shook her head. "We can't talk about this in the hallway."

Jess was turning away as I grabbed her arm. "Yes, we can."

Scorn in her eyes, she looked down at my hand and I let it drop. It'd been a bad move on my part.

"Fine." Her chest heaved as she took a deep breath. "The space outside the radio station is way too open and there are too many variables. That's just asking for trouble."

"It's what the fans are asking for."

She pursed her lips. "You're looking at this the wrong way."

"Yeah? What's the right way?"

"Put yourself in the mindset of a crazed woman fan, not a normal person, a stalker."

"Why would I want to do that?"

"Because what you think is reasonable is irrelevant. It's what this person thinks and does that matters."

I reached for her shoulder. "Jess, I'm not going to do anything stupid."

She shook me off. "That doesn't change the fact that this would be the perfect time for the stalker to get to you and maybe take things a step further. I trust my gut on this, Lachie."

"Look, it's not going to end in disaster. This is just a small gig. It won't finish up like Ariana Grande's concert in Manchester."

"You're not listening, Lachie. You don't know what's going through your stalker's mind, what she thinks god might tell her to do, or when she might escalate things."

I paced the floor, raked a hand through my hair. "I can't live this way. I can't plan every move and consider everything from a safety point of view. I can't stay home for the rest of my life. I'm already taking precautions. Isn't that enough? Damn it, I never wanted a bodyguard in the first place."

Regret flooded through me as soon as the words slipped out. Jess's eyes widened, her lower lip quivering, I was sure of it, only for a split second before she composed herself.

I took her hands into mine. She didn't resist. Didn't do much of anything.

"I'm sorry," I said. "I didn't mean it that way."

"I know." She cleared her throat to hide the quaver from her voice as she looked up at me. "Back at your parents' house, you said you were more aware of what was going on. It's not true. You're kidding yourself."

This was more than just an argument. If she trusted her instincts, so did I. Something rumbled deep inside me, like the first tremors of an earthquake, and it was only the beginning. No turning back.

I threw my hands up. "Don't you get it? I like having you here but this isn't going to work if I can't be myself and play guitar and do all the regular things I do."

"But you're not *regular*. You play in a rock band."

"Look, I'm not asking for something outrageous. In my world, this is perfectly normal. I do a radio interview. I play a few songs. It's no major drama."

"But it is. That performance in the square outside is a huge problem."

"That's where you're wrong. This isn't about my safety. This is about trust."

A little piece of my heart broke off as I said the words. My own words, I couldn't deny them.

Jess had said I wasn't aware, and she was so wrong because I was aware of everything that was happening, the stutter in my heart as it tried to right itself, the emotion glittering in her eyes as she held herself together, and the depth of this discussion. Because trust was everything.

"I have a lot of faith in you, Lachie, in a lot of ways," she said. "You write beautiful songs, you're a great guitar player and, most importantly, you're a good person. You just don't want anyone else to see it."

"You've seen it."

"We're different, you and me. You've grown up in an environment where you've been nurtured, not bullied, and your creative side has flourished. You know a lot about music but you're not an expert in personal security."

"What's that got to do with it?"

Her gray eyes wide, she stared. "How can I respect your decisions? How can I be with you when you don't care enough about your safety? You've told me all about who you are and how you want to live your life." She spread her arms. "Well, this is me. Martial arts, personal safety, close protection. This is what I do. It's a part of me just as much as music is a part of you."

My heart crumbling, I sucked in a deep breath even though I knew it wasn't going to make me feel better.

The irony was killing me. I'd always thought that if I loved someone—deep romantic love, the real thing—that

I'd lose a part of myself. But it wasn't like that at all. It had happened. I'd fallen in love. And it had made me whole.

Whereas now a part of me was gone. And there was no fixing it.

"You always think the worst of people," I said.

"That's not true."

"Only of me, then."

She opened her mouth to deny it and couldn't do it, couldn't tell me I was wrong, couldn't make things up to me anymore than I could to her. I might've been mistaken about a lot of things in the past but not about this. As much as I despised the position we'd ended up in, I'd spoken the truth.

"We can't do this. You can't do it either, not if what you've said is true." I turned away, then stopped. "You're good at your job and I need a bodyguard. Let's keep things simple. Let's just keep it … professional."

And another little piece of my heart broke away.

CHAPTER SIXTEEN

Jess

I was a bodyguard. It was what I'd always wanted to be and exactly what I didn't want to be.

Every day was dragging me down, but I stayed upright and alert. Somehow. Awareness was my number one weapon, the thing that put me ahead of the game, because I trusted my gut and could anticipate problems before they happened. I had good instincts.

And I didn't have Lachie, not anymore. Maybe I'd never really had him. Maybe I'd been kidding myself.

The parcel in my hand, I grabbed a pair of scissors and some rubber gloves from the kitchen and bounded for the dining table. I cut the string from the package and made a neat hole in the brown paper wrapping so I could pull out what lay beneath, a gift of some sort wrapped in sparkly purple paper covered with balloons.

The shiny paper might be covered in fingerprints, more prints for the police to add to their collection, but they weren't much good without a person to match them to.

Footsteps behind me. It was too late to hide.

I turned, standing between the table and Lachie. "You don't need to see this."

He raised his eyebrows. "Another wedding invitation?"

"Something like that. I'll take a—"

"I can handle it."

The hardness in his voice sent a shiver up my spine. I wanted to tell him I wasn't the enemy, that the problem wasn't me, that the trouble lay with his stalker.

Except he wouldn't believe me and there was no point going there. I'd already screwed up and then compounded that mistake by staying here.

Because I couldn't bear to leave. Instead, I clung to the fragments of what had once been a relationship, but wasn't even that anymore. It was *professional*. Yet still I stayed.

So perhaps Lachie could stay too. He was a big boy, after all.

I peeled the packaging tape from the gift, then pulled apart the sides of the purple paper. A hand-written white card lay on the top:

God is giving us the child we always wanted. We will be married or there will be blood.

Lachie stayed beside me. Didn't move. I couldn't even hear him breathing.

I put the card to one side and picked up a neatly folded, pale pink newborn's bodysuit. Another body suit was underneath, this one pale blue, slashed and covered in blood. A bloodied knife lay on top.

Talk about screwed up. The stalker wanted to play happy families and was making threats at the same time. Whatever way you looked at it, her fantasy world was becoming more complex and convoluted, more intense and deranged.

Beside me, Lachie spluttered. I should've been taking care of him first and everything else second. Guilt flooded through me. Maybe he was right and I was too much of a bodyguard, always thinking the worst of people. Of him.

No, I'd never thought the worst of Lachie. I was the one being realistic. Because one of us had to be. Besides, that was the reason I was here. And now, it was the reason Lachie and I couldn't be together in the way we had before.

Disgusted, he turned to me. "So now this ... this person thinks we're getting married and having a baby? This is fucked."

I'd already tried to explain that stalkers weren't rational but he didn't seem to be listening, yet another of the problems that lay between us. Still, I felt for him. He didn't deserve this, any of it.

"It is crazy," I said. "That's the whole point. What your stalker thinks and does isn't necessarily going to make sense to the rest of us."

He was standing beside me, only inches away, inches that felt like miles. It came back to me, the way he'd made my senses sizzle, his hands all over my body and mine all over his.

And more than that, the way he'd made me feel whole and loved and wanted. On the inside. It had been all encompassing—our two lives becoming wrapped up together, living under one roof, two hearts pulsing together.

Except it had never been love on his part.

We couldn't be together, something he'd made abundantly clear. I couldn't do it anyway, couldn't lose a part of myself to have him back again. Yet that did nothing to change the longing in my heart.

I reached for his arm, my fingertips brushing the bare skin, stretching toward his hand.

He pulled away.

I was fooling myself. Again. Damn it, how many times was I going to be knocked to the ground before I recognized the truth? Tears burned at the back of my eyes but I held them back, hoped they didn't show.

"I can ask Andrew to get someone else to take over." I kept the quaver from my voice. "Would that be better?"

"No." He held my gaze but I couldn't read what was in the depths of his green eyes. There was a time I'd thought I knew him. A pang cut through my heart and I couldn't understand how something that had felt so right could simply disappear.

"Okay."

I lied. It wasn't okay. Nothing was okay, not the stalker's increasingly weird behavior, not the upcoming radio show, and certainly not the way things were with Lachie.

Couldn't he see the desperation dripping inside me?

I wanted things to be the way they were before, but that was never going to happen.

CHAPTER SEVENTEEN

Lachie

We were back at the damn hospital again. I couldn't wait to see the end of this place, yet there was no way I could let my dad know how pissed I was about this and a lot of other things in my life.

At least this time, the doctors believed they'd got to the root of my father's latest problem. Dad had gotten through everything, only to end up in pain again—agony, actually—after his intestines had dropped and become twisted. It seemed it wasn't enough for him to have cancer and a colostomy bag. He had to have every possible complication as well.

He was supposed to have been getting better but when I looked at him, slumped in yet another hospital bed, he didn't seem very damn healthy to me. He'd lost so much weight that all that was left was sagging flesh and bones. Mom had already told me this was only to be expected, that he wouldn't bounce back overnight. It'd take time.

Standing by his bed, I gripped his hand, didn't want to let go.

Dad flinched, tried to get his hand away. "Hey, watch

it."

I loosened my grasp. "Sorry."

He waved it off with his other hand, which appeared to be functioning just fine. "I'm too old for arm wrestling."

Sounded like Dad's sense of humor was coming back to him. Maybe he was getting better after all.

Through the corner of my eye, I saw Jess moving, probably checking the door or hallway. It was good to know she was there. Despite everything, I appreciated the moral support, more than appreciated it, because I'd probably fall apart without it.

I didn't want anyone else to see me this way with my father and I sure as hell didn't want another bodyguard. Things were hard enough as they were without having to explain my situation to someone else all over again.

Funny, though, that as much as I needed her, it hurt to have here.

"I'll leave you and Mom to it then," I said to Dad. "You might be able to get some rest if I stop bothering you."

Serious now. "You're never a bother, Lachie. You're the best son a man could have, but you've got your own life. I understand."

And he was the best dad I could hope for. My throat tight, I leaned over, ready to hold him and not let him go for a long time.

He scrunched up his face, held a hand out. "No, no. You'll probably break something. Give your mom an extra long hug. She'll appreciate it."

Even when he was down, he could still make me smile. "Okay."

I wondered if he really felt that delicate or if he simply didn't want the attention. He'd never liked a lot of fuss, yet he seemed to surrounded by the stuff thanks to his current condition. Which was getting better. I had to believe that. The doctors didn't give fake hopes or diagnoses and they'd been up front with everything so far.

I held my arms out to my mom. She came to me, resting her head on my chest while I held her and rubbed her back.

Eventually, she let go. "I remember when you used to be smaller than me, and look at you now."

"That was a while ago, Mom." I turned to Dad. "Was that extra-long enough? I hope I did okay in the hug department."

"You did, son."

By the time I looked at Mom again, she was reaching out to Jess, wrapping her arms around her. Jess hugged her right back and for that one second that her eyes were pressed shut, I didn't see a bodyguard. I saw the little girl she must once have been, someone who needed hugs and nourishment and love. I swallowed the lump in my throat.

They broke off the embrace and the moment was gone. Still, I was sure I hadn't imagined it.

Jess glanced outside the doorway, then stepped back inside, leaned over, and handed me the bag from the floor. I was finally returning to the teen ward with band merchandise. Those kids needed The Merchants' CDs and T-shirts and posters. And good health, they needed that most of all.

We strode down the hallway together, stopping to wait for the elevator at the far end. Hospitals were full of endless corridors.

A dull ache throbbed deep inside. Maybe it was my dad or the sick kids we were about to visit or maybe it was seeing Jess with my mom. Whatever the reason, I had to get it off my chest.

I looked at Jess. "I'm sorry for what happened yesterday."

"With the baby clothes? It's not your fault you've got a stalker."

"Not just that." I had to spit it out. "I'm sorry I was so short with you. You're only trying to help. You *are* helping and it means a lot to me. There aren't a lot of people I'd trust to see me with my dad when he's in such a bad way."

There was that word again. Trust.

"I hope he's getting better," she said. "Truly I do."

"Thanks, but what I'm saying is that we need to try to get along a bit better."

She nodded. "Sure, we can do that."

"I-I don't want a different bodyguard."

I want *you*. But I couldn't add the last part, couldn't lead her along. I also couldn't let go.

The doors opened, the elevator empty, so we got in.

Jess pressed the button, the doors closing again. "It was lovely, what your dad said to you."

"What was that?"

"About you being the best son he could hope for. Your parents are good people. You've got strong roots."

And she had airhead parents who'd gone off to California and left her with her aunt and uncle. She'd only been sixteen, still a kid.

The doors opened and we headed for the teen ward. Somehow all the shitty things in my life felt like they were falling on top of me—Dad's cancer, the whole stalker thing, the wedding invitations, the bloodied baby clothes, and bullet cartridges.

Time to forget about all that and think about the kids I was about to visit because they deserved better than they were getting. I could brighten their day. I could do this one small thing.

I said hello to the nurses at the desk, to Michelle, the only one I knew by name, as we made our way toward the female section.

There was one kid in particular I wanted to see today, one guy who'd made an impression and touched my heart. Sometimes you made a special connection with someone and this was one of those times. So I was saving the best for last. Brandon.

I'd brought along some Pixies' CDs and a couple of tickets to The Flats Festival. Unfortunately, it was too soon to get hold of backstage passes but I could send those on later.

Walking into the girls' ward, I was hit with, "Oh my god, it's Lachie Tyler again. I can't believe it!"

I smiled, remembering this girl from before. "Are you still here?"

She nodded, her eyes ready to burst from their sockets. "I'm getting out tomorrow but I'm so glad I'm here today. My friends won't believe I'm seeing you a second time."

A part of me wished she was back home and healthy, and part of me was glad to be bringing some excitement to her day. That was the thing about seeing sick kids. I was always so torn and, without fail, it always brought me back down to earth.

Jess stayed in the background, as she always did. It pained me that I needed a bodyguard, that she had to be here at all. I wanted her to stay and I wanted her to go, both at the same time, none of which made sense.

We made our way through to the boys' ward, giving out Merchants' CDs, caps, posters, and other merchandise along the way. To see the looks on some of the kids' faces, you'd think I'd given them a million dollars. It made my day.

I walked into the last room, the one Brandon shared with three other boys. Only he wasn't there. Instead, there was another kid in Brandon's bed.

And I knew.

Despair flooded my heart. I told myself he must've been sent home but somehow I could feel the truth deep in my gut.

I didn't dare ask any of these boys what had happened to Brandon, didn't want to hear it from the lips of another teenager who was so sick himself. Instead, I pretended everything was normal and talked to the four boys like I'd talked to everyone else.

Jess looked at me, didn't say anything. The bag I was holding was now empty except for the Pixies' CDs and tickets. I gripped it in one hand and grabbed Jess's hand with the other, hurtling us toward the nurses' station.

I let go of her and leaned over the counter. "Excuse me, Michelle."

A bright smile on her face. "What can I help you with?"

"There was a boy in the last bed over there, Brandon. Can you tell me what happened to him? I've got some stuff for him and I want to get in touch."

Her face fell. "I'm sorry, Lachie."

It hit me like a punch to the gut. Sucked the air right

out of me. I'd been right. And I wished I wasn't.

"Brandon didn't make it," she said.

How the fuck was this fair? What kind of world was this?

"I don't get it," I said. "He was so bright, so happy, such a with-it kid."

"It happens that way sometimes. It's as if they get a final burst of energy so they can say goodbye to everyone and then we lose them. He went downhill very quickly that night after you left."

But I hadn't been saying goodbye to him. That wasn't what it had been about. He was just a kid. He should've been playing his guitar and starting a band, doing homework and studying for exams, dating girls and taking someone special to the prom. He should've been doing anything else except dying.

We walked away. I wasn't even sure where we were going anymore. Out in the corridor, Jess pressed the button for the elevator.

"I'm sorry," she said.

She brushed her hand against mine as we got in the elevator, then gave my hand a squeeze as we shuffled in, joining four or five people who were already in there. She didn't speak as we got out, and that was exactly what I needed—for her to not speak—because my eyes were burning, my head aching, throat tight, and I didn't want to lose it. Not here. Not anywhere.

Jess led me across an open path that led to the parking garage opposite the hospital. She was keeping her eye out, which seemed to be the story of her life, and also meant I didn't need to worry so much.

Two guys were heading our way, when one of them

stopped in the middle of the path and called my name. Probably just fans but I couldn't handle this and we had to get past them to get to the car.

"Keep moving," Jess said under her breath, then more loudly to the guy, "Sorry, sir, this is a bad time. I hope you'll—"

"But that's Lachie Fucking Tyler!" he yelled.

"Please let us pass, *sir*." The way she said 'sir' made it sound more like shithead.

The guy didn't move, still blocking the path. Then he reached for my arm. Big mistake.

Jess shoved her hand in his face and stepped past him, tossing him to the ground in some sort of judo throw, while his friend looked on in shock. She took it all in her stride, simply kept going as if nothing had happened. Left the guy on the ground moaning and muttering under his breath.

At any other time, this would've made me smile. The guy was twice her size and she'd thrown him. How cool was that? Awesome, in fact. But today I didn't feel like smiling. The guy's timing couldn't have been worse.

I didn't even know what was going on anymore.

CHAPTER EIGHTEEN

Jess

Lachie and Nick were in their element being interviewed on the radio. Nick took on a front-man persona, quite different from the guy I'd seen before, and Lachie was easygoing and natural. His own man.

I had a good view into the soundproof booth in which they were sitting. Meanwhile audio was being projected into this adjoining room, as well as into the square outside the building.

Stepping over to the window, I checked out the crowd that had gathered. Teenage girls outnumbered the rest by far, but it was still a mixed lot with people of all ages, even some with gray hair. I had to admire them for still having the energy for this sort of thing. Maybe it was a sign of just how much The Merchants' music meant to them.

Shifting my gaze, I peered into the booth. I could see what the listeners couldn't, the smile on the radio host's face. You'd think Aspen was meeting her idols, and maybe she was.

Lachie and Nick sat on the other side of the desk from her, both of them relaxed with guitars on their laps and headphones covering their ears.

"Do you have one more song for us?" Aspen asked.

"Sure," Lachie said. "This one's an old favorite called *Too Much Trouble*, but it's not of course. Nothing's too much trouble for you, Aspen."

A pang of jealousy cut through me at his easy banter. It shouldn't, but it did.

I knew the song right away, though it sounded different done acoustically in the studio with just the two of them, rougher and readier. Lachie belted out the introduction on the guitar, then held back as Nick came in with the vocals, his voice harsh and husky. I liked the imperfection of it.

The song finished and the host asked them another question. From inside the soundproof booth, they couldn't hear the clapping and cheering from outside.

Originally, the station had planned for Lachie and Nick to perform a short acoustic set in the square, but Andrew and I had talked the two of them out of it. Too dangerous given we had a stalker on the loose. I'd have talked Lachie out of the radio interview too if I'd been able. Instead, I had to settle for harm minimization.

Andrew was waiting outside the building to join us as soon as we were ready, and one of his guys was stationed on the other side of the door. We'd upgraded security for today with a visible presence outside as well as several guys who were blending into the crowd.

Aspen asked, "So what's the secret to your success?"

"Beer," Nick said. "Plenty of beer."

The three of them laughed. I had to hand it to them.

"Actually," Lachie said, "we're very lucky to be able to make a living doing something we love. Because we love making music. For me, personally, it was great that I fell in with such a great bunch of guys. Makes life a lot easier."

"Can you tell us about Austin Murphy leaving the band?" Aspen asked.

"Ah, the cutting edge journalist questions." Lachie laughed it off. "Austin's got a rockabilly outfit together, The Detonators. You should check them out. In fact, I think you should have them on the show. What do you say?"

"We might just do that. Tell me, how are you enjoying being back in Frankston?"

"Well, I feel I should click my heels together and say there's nowhere like home," Lachie said, hamming it up.

Nick added, "It's wonderful to be back. We've all got families here. Frankston was a great place to grow up. Still is. There's always that feeling that you can make anything happen here."

For me, Frankston had the best and the worst of everything. It was where I got beaten up on the bus as a kid and it was also where I found kickboxing and a new home with my aunt and uncle. It was where I found myself, if I was going to be honest.

By the time Aspen brought the interview to an end she'd already gone half an hour overtime. I stared out of the window. While they'd been talking and playing songs, the crowd outside had built up. Hopefully they wouldn't be too disgruntled by the wait.

Lachie and Nick came out of the studio, both of them smiling as they chatted and placed their guitars in their respective cases. The room was secure and we'd arranged for someone to collect their guitars shortly.

First things first, though. We had to escort the two of

them into the square and make sure they were safe while they signed autographs and talked to the fans. They'd make jokes, have their photos taken, make people feel at home, and then we could leave.

The other guard led the way to the elevator, ushered us in, then stepped out to check the foyer before motioning for us to follow. Lachie and Nick both seemed pumped after the interview, and the banter seemed to come to them naturally. It was the sort of thing the crowd outside would love.

Not all of us could be relaxed, though. I wouldn't be able to unwind until well after this was over.

Andrew waited by the glass doors at the entrance. A big guy, he was hard to miss at the best of times. He turned to greet us, his trademark huge smile missing, because he was at work now.

The area outside had been cordoned off, leaving a wide path for Nick and Lachie while they were walking through the gauntlet. A wide foot-route with lots of white space was important for security.

I'd already briefed the two of them about how they should stand two or more feet back so people had to reach out to them, and Lachie and Nick would then have to extend their arms to make contact. This way they could touch the fans' hands without letting anyone get a firm grip.

As we stepped outside, Nick headed straight for the crowd, a security guy by his side. He stepped in close, way too close to the fans, and started shaking hands with them right away.

Great, he was ignoring everything I'd told him. My blood boiled.

A girl leapt across and kissed him on the cheek. The guard pushed her back, not rough, just firm enough. Meanwhile, Nick grinned. I could see from his body language that he was telling the guard it was okay. It wasn't okay, and that was exactly what the guard was trying to explain.

"Don't get close," I said to Lachie.

"I got it."

He swallowed, his Adam's apple bobbing up and down. I had a feeling he was finally starting to take his own security seriously.

He reached for my hand, gave it a squeeze, then let go. Beside us, Andrew didn't miss a trick. He saw the movement, small though it was, then looked at me and out across the crowd.

The two of us on either side of Lachie, we stepped forward to the sound of swooning to our left. Lachie chatted to the girls who'd taken pride of position near the door, took their hands into his. From a distance. Just like we'd told him.

I scanned the crowd on both sides of the cordon, knowing most attacks were close, most likely within twenty feet or so. That covered quite an area and there were a lot of people here.

I spotted a familiar face, someone I'd seen before, less than ten feet ahead standing by the cordon. Ordinary looking, brown hair pulled back from her face. Something was different from before. I wasn't sure what.

Lachie's attention was elsewhere. A middle-aged woman in front of him had wrapped a scarf over her head but without any hair peeping out from underneath. No eyebrows either. Probably a cancer patient and exactly the sort of person to tug at Lachie's heartstrings. She was holding her right arm out to him.

He sidled closer to me. "Is it okay?"

"Yes, just be quick."

I knew exactly what he had in mind. And I couldn't stop him from being Lachie.

He reached out to her. "Forget the handshake. You need a hug."

Following my instincts, I stepped in, closer to Lachie and to the crowd.

A flash of recognition. I knew where I'd seen the familiar woman before. At Charlie's Guitars and Records.

I headed in her direction.

A flicker of movement. Her hand reaching into the tote bag on her shoulder. Her eyes on Lachie.

And I knew.

Only action, no thought. I leapt across. Her hand came out of the bag. A gun. My heart rate spiked. She couldn't see me. For her, there was only Lachie. Her target.

"Gun!" I yelled.

I was there in an instant. Both her hands gripped the gun. I grabbed her wrist, her hands, pointed the gun toward the ground.

It went off. Deafening.

Control the gun, control the attacker.

A head butt, my only weapon. I slammed my forehead onto the bridge of her nose. Blood spurted out. She moaned, crumpled to the ground. The gun slipped from her fingers. In my hands now.

Suddenly Andrew was there and I passed him the gun. He had the woman on the ground, his knee on her back. She wasn't going anywhere. There was no one I could trust for this more than him. I straightened.

Lachie… Two security guys were on either side of him. The same with Nick further ahead in the crowd.

Screaming filled the air. It was as if the mute button in my head got turned off. I'd shoved people aside to get to the woman, knocked the cordon over. People were distressed, backing off, trying to get away.

We were through the worst. I hoped. I still had to make sure Lachie was safe. No time to relax. No time at all.

Suddenly. Ahead of me. Danger. Coming my way. Snarling. Eyes blazing. A tall skinny guy pushed two girls aside, headed straight for me.

"You hurt her."

Why was he even saying that?

His fist. Coming straight at me. I slipped my head out of the way. His hand scraped the side of my ear. So close.

Not over. I slammed a left hook into his jaw, then a right. Gave him no room to move.

Not enough. I slid my hands to the back of his neck, yanked his head down, rammed in the knees. He dropped to the ground, clutching his head.

Not over. I had to get to Lachie. Had to make sure he'd gotten out of here safely.

I ran straight down the gauntlet to the car. One of the security guys held the door open for me, slammed it shut as soon as I got in.

The car lurched away. Tires screeched. The momentum had me glued to the rear seat.

Lachie looked across at me, his eyes filled with fear or relief or both. He didn't say anything, just reached across and pulled me into his arms. The only place I wanted to

be. Tears burned at the back of my eyes. I held them back.
Safe, that was all I cared about.

CHAPTER NINETEEN

Lachie

Two days and about twenty thousand hours of police interviews later—or at least that was what it felt like—I finally had the chance to talk to Jess again. Properly.

The police had filled me in. My stalker had a name, Alicia Jones, a real name because it sure as hell wasn't Angel. She was a direct match for the fingerprints and DNA. She'd been in and out of psychiatric institutions since she was in her teens, and she was back in one now. Normally medication helped keep her condition under control but, for whatever reason, she'd stopped taking the drugs and started hallucinating. According to her, god had told her we should be together.

Though she'd been charged, it wasn't certain yet whether she'd end up in jail or an institution because of her psychiatric problems. Her parents had flown in from Connecticut to take care of her and were hoping to take her back to live with them. The other side of the country seemed like a good place for her to be.

And the guy who'd attacked Jess had been her boyfriend. Not that he had a mental condition, other than being an asshole. There were assault charges for him too.

I pressed the buzzer outside the building where Jess lived. Since there was no more stalker, there was no need for her to stay at my place, so she'd moved back to the apartment she shared with another girl. And my house felt empty.

"Come on up," she said through the intercom. "Third floor."

Hearing the click of the door release, I strode in and waited for the elevator. In the last couple of days, I'd been going through a lot of things in my head. And my heart.

The elevator doors opened. Empty. I stepped inside.

My dad was back at home and his mood had picked up greatly. He was over the worst of it. That was what the doctors told us and what my dad kept reminding me. I had to believe it.

He was faring a lot better than Brandon had. I'd only known that young man for about five minutes but grief still gripped me when I thought of him. He'd given me some ideas, even if ideas was all they were at the moment—for some sort of trust for teen cancer survivors or maybe for medical research. I was going do something even if I didn't know exactly what.

The elevator doors opened and I strode down the corridor, then knocked on the door of number thirty-three.

One thing I knew for sure. Life was fragile. You had to keep living it, making the most of every day. Life was too short to leave love behind.

Jess opened the door and the breath left my body. She was everything I'd ever wanted.

Banging and crashing sounds rang through the air.

"What's that?"

"Come on in." She pulled the door wider.

I stepped inside where half the living room was taken up by a Gretsch round badge kit with a skinny, dark haired girl behind it. Big drum kit, tiny girl.

"Meet Holly," Jess said.

She gave me a quick drum roll and looked up. "Hi."

I nodded. "Ah, the classic 60s Gretsch drum kit in mother of toilet seat!"

She shot me a dirty look. "It's white marine pearl, thank you very much. The same stuff Gretsch use for their sparkle jets."

"So you know a thing or two about guitars?"

"I know a lot more about drums."

Holly launched into a paradiddle, followed by a shuffle, then straight into some four on the floor. It would've been a lot louder without the practice pads.

"Yep, I'm convinced," I yelled.

Jess nudged me. "I told you it was noisy at my place."

Holly got up and shook my hand rather vigorously. "I was away when Jess was staying at your place, but I'm back now. I'm so thrilled to meet you." She wouldn't let go of my hand.

I looked down. "I can tell."

She let go. "Oh, sorry."

"Maybe we should go somewhere," Jess suggested.

Holly's face fell. "Are you trying to get rid of me? I only just met him."

"We could go for a walk," I said. "There's a park on the corner."

Jess screwed up her face. "You? Go for a walk?"

I pointed to the baseball cap on my head. "Sure, I'm

wearing my disguise. Lovely meeting you, Holly. Promise we can talk next time."

Jess and I headed out the door.

CHAPTER TWENTY

Jess

"I'm done working as a bodyguard," I said when we reached the park.

Lachie stopped, shock in his eyes. "Really?"

I nodded. "Really. I'm going to do what I've always wanted to do."

As we started walking again, he asked. "What's that?"

"Remember how you thought it was strange that I used to be a kindergarten teacher?"

"Yeah."

"It's not so weird. I want to open my own martial arts school, something that combines two things I'm good at—teaching and kickboxing. I want to focus on classes for kids and teenagers, so that other young people can get what I did out of martial arts."

"That's fantastic. You should absolutely do it."

I'd probably still have to do some security work to help make ends meet and possibly some relief teaching too, all of which was fine by me, now I was on the right path.

"You're an amazing bodyguard, though," Lachie said.

"You know that, don't you? You're the best, Jess, and I can vouch for that with my life."

We'd come a long way. Lachie had already thanked me about a thousand times.

But it wasn't enough for me to keep doing something because I was good at it. I had to be true to myself.

For me, this meant I had to look after myself as well as others. And I didn't want my life to revolve around the stalkers and crazies in the world when there were so many positive things I could focus on.

I wasn't a fourteen-year-old girl getting beaten up on the bus anymore. I was a woman and I trusted my gut more than ever. I could trust Lachie too. I could open my heart to him and if he rejected me, that was how it had to be. But I couldn't live the rest of my life wondering 'what-if' about the two of us.

I stopped in the shade of a tree, trying to gather the courage to tell him how I felt. Why was this so much harder than neutralizing a gun-toting stalker and fighting off her psycho boyfriend? Why were feelings so much harder than the physical?

Lachie took my hands into his. "I don't know how we came to this."

My lower lip trembled. Because I didn't know either.

He pulled me closer. "There's something I should have said a long time ago."

That sucked the air right out of me. I didn't dare think it… Couldn't bear it…

"You're shaking," he said.

I opened my mouth to speak but the words wouldn't come.

"I love you, Jess."

Tears started steaming down my face. I couldn't work out what was happening. I wasn't sentimental. I didn't cry.

"And I want us to be together." He wrapped his arms around me, held me in his arms while I whimpered like a baby.

After a while, he held me at arm's length, looked into my eyes.

"Well, that's handy," I said, my voice quavering. "Because I love you too."

He pressed his lips against mine and I finally stopped shaking. This was only the beginning. We'd have tomorrow and the next day and the day after that. We'd have the lives we wanted to build for ourselves.

A future was a wonderful thing.

Keep reading for a sneak preview of Book 4…

ACKNOWLEDGMENTS

First of all, a big thanks to my very own rock star and in-house consultant, James.

Thanks very much to the people I interviewed, all experts in your particular fields and very patient with my dumb questions—Jenny Kim, Brooke Lundy, Scott Wilson, Brendan Murphy and Jo Taylor. Thanks heaps, guys!

And of course thanks to my fabulous critique partners, Claire, Lorraine, Juanita, Teena and Anna.

ABOUT THE AUTHOR

Susanna Rogers is the author of rock star romances for adults and kick butt books for young adults. Inspired by her very own in-house rock star and years of going to gigs, she penned the Mosh Series after writing and releasing several young adult novels. She's also a kickboxer and dreams of empowering girls and guys around the globe to believe in themselves, to take care and follow their own dreams. She has a soft spot for romantic suspense, also with kick butt heroines, so you never know what might be coming up next.

She would love to hear from you—susannarogers.com.

If you like her books, please post a review on Amazon or Goodreads. She'd like that a lot.

LIGHT & SHADE
MOSH BOOK 4

CHAPTER ONE

Joel

Desperation wasn't a good look, not when you wanted something and certainly not when you were dealing with guys who were so damn successful. People could smell it, often from a distance, and it wasn't an attractive aroma.

Act cool, Joel. Yeah, right, like that was going to happen.

It'd been over a month since word had got out that The Merchants' bass player was leaving, a month of putting my feelers out and talking to anyone who even vaguely knew the guys. And waiting. A hell of a lot of waiting.

So when I found out about tonight, I'd jumped at the chance, made sure I got on the invitation list. I'd been playing in bands for ten years, ever since I was seventeen, playing my guts out, shitty gigs and good gigs, always hoping to make it in the music industry even though I had a 'real' job.

This could be my big chance. Maybe my only chance. And I had to make it happen because no one else was going to do it for me.

Lachie Tyler knew how to put on a party, that was for sure. Once I'd managed to get in. The security guys out the front were a bit over the top, but maybe that was what happened when you were famous. Like buying a huge house. It looked like he hadn't got around to buying much furniture yet, but the place was so packed with people you could hardly notice.

I'd seen Lachie heading toward the back of the house earlier, so that was where I should go too. Better to do this sooner than later.

I turned. And saw her. Short blond hair, head tilted, and looking right at me. A crimson, off-the-shoulder top showed off pretty shoulders, her arms folded pushing up her boobs, so they might've been staring at me too.

The hair on the back of my neck stood on end. In a good way. The best way possible. All my senses left me, just like that.

"You look like a guy who needs a drink." She swiped a long neck from a passing waiter and shoved it into my hand.

"Thanks."

I drank some beer. Tried to compose myself. Wondered if she'd been watching me. Was it even possible a woman like her could be checking *me* out?

"Nothing tastes as good as free beer." I took another long gulp, embarrassed because that was the best I could come up with, which was weird. Not my normal self at all. Must be nerves. I should speak to Lachie. Soon. Get it over with. Then I'd be back. Oh yeah, I'd be right back.

She smiled, her warm brown eyes lighting up. "I'm Scarlett."

"Such a pretty name." At least I got one thing right.

A skinny young thing shoved me aside, her arms outstretched to Scarlett as she dived between us and wrapped her arms around the young woman I'd barely met. Then a guy appeared. Did the same thing.

Scarlett was all smiles, returning their hugs, happy to see them. In fact, she looked like she'd forgotten about me in a few short seconds. Disappointment washed through me.

And brought me to my senses. What was I thinking? This thing with The Merchants could be the chance of a lifetime and I'd gotten so easily distracted. Man, she was one hell of a distraction.

I took a deep breath. I could catch up with her later. In fact, I'd make sure of it. It wasn't every day a woman as stunning has her introduced herself to me. Not every day a woman made me lose my shit either.

No more deliberation. I forced myself to leave, weaving my way through the crowd as I headed toward the back of the house.

Bar staff had set themselves up at the outdoor kitchen. A waiter took my empty beer from me, handed me another one. Like magic. I was going to need it.

Seemed to be more furniture out here than inside the house. A few people had gathered around the outdoor sofas set up to one side of the yard while others were hanging around long table on the patio. Looked like the perfect place to have a beer with a few friends on a summer's evening like tonight, except in this case there were more than a few friends. The place was filling up.

I liked a party as much as the next guy, but was comfortable on my own too, probably because I'd spent lots of time alone as a kid. Too much. Still, I was better off not living alone and would need to start looking for a new roommate soon.

Deep in conversation with someone, Lachie had his back to me. I swallowed, a fresh wave of anxiety surging through me. I had a lot riding on this.

Should I interrupt? Introduce myself? What if I blew it?

The Merchants of Menace weren't just any band. This was my dream band, what I'd always wanted but had never even dared admit to myself because it seemed too surreal and too far out of my reach.

Now they needed a bass player. This was meant to be. It had to be.

Squealing sounds came from the hot tub at the rear of the yard. "Lachie, Lachie!"

Two naked girls sat up, waving wildly. My eyes nearly popped out of my head. I couldn't believe it. Charlotte Banks. I'd kissed her in the ninth grade, but she hadn't looked like that back then. Talk about way too much information. It felt like my teenage dreams were coming back to haunt me.

Hell, I had to get that image out of my head and do what I'd come out here to do and talk to Lachie Tyler.

He looked away, embarrassed. My big chance. I strode toward him, just a few steps, hard ones to take. Nerves shot through me, my throat suddenly tight.

I shook his hand. "Great party. We've met before."

A blank look on his face. "Have we?"

"Joel Hitchcock." If I'd expected by some miracle he'd remember me, I was wrong. "From Black Paisley." Not even a flicker of recognition from Lachie, so I said, "The band."

Each time I added something, a small piece of my remaining self-confidence got chipped away. And soon I wouldn't have Black Paisley anymore. One of the guys was leaving, our lead singer was drugged up half the time, and the band was falling apart.

I should've known better. We'd been thrilled Lachie had come along to one of our gigs all those years ago, even if it hadn't been our gig exactly. We'd been the support act, and his presence had been a big deal to us. Not to him. And that figured.

Still, I couldn't stop here. I had to at least try, so I told Lachie how I played a bit of guitar and piano and a lot of bass. Shit, I shouldn't have mentioned the other instruments. I should have stuck with the bass because that was the whole point. He was polite though, I had to hand it to him, even told me I was versatile like Nick, their singer.

Despite the compliment, my heart was sinking every step of the way. The look on Lachie's face told me he was going through the motions. Meanwhile the ache inside me deepened, despite the fact I was still hoping for the best, reaching and grasping for this thing I'd never be able to have.

"Lots of guys play bass just so they can get a gig," he said. "Someone told me years ago that if you're a bass player, you'll always get a gig whereas everyone wants to be the guitar player. I reckon that still holds true."

But I played bass because it felt right, because I could write the songs and the bass lines I wanted to play. Because it was me.

I had to give it one last shot. "I, uh, heard you guys might be after a bass player."

Desperation dripped from my voice, so thick even I could hear it. It pooled inside me too because now I was so close—or so far—it confirmed just how badly I wanted this.

"We might have already found someone," he said.

My stomach plummeted. "Really, who's that?"

"A guy called Domino."

I gritted my teeth. Of all the bass players in the world, of all the musicians in Frankston, they had to choose him.

Lachie raised his eyebrow. "You know him?"

"You could say that."

This was typical. Domino could talk his way into anything. He'd stolen my girlfriend from me, talked his way right into her pants and her heart, and it might've been years ago but I hadn't forgotten. I couldn't.

Anyway, wasn't he in rehab? Or had he just come out? My head spinning, I couldn't even remember.

It took all my strength not to say anything. I'd only make myself look bad. Or worse, I'd end up ranting and that was not a good look. Besides, Lachie didn't know me from a bar of soap and had no reason to believe anything I said, not when he already had a bass player.

I swallowed back the resentment, wondering what the hell to say next.

Scarlett came toward us, gliding through the crowd. She'd stand out anywhere with her pale hair, that bright top and that attitude. My heart melted at the sight of her. Such magnificent timing.

She greeted Lachie with a kiss on the cheek. A pang of jealousy shot through me. At a kiss on the cheek? Talk about crazy.

"This is some house you've got," she said.

Maybe that was what I should've done too, flattered Lachie a little, found some common ground. It wouldn't have been hard since I was a huge fan of The Merchants.

Scarlett placed her hands on her hips. "You've got so much house and it's so empty."

Something we agreed on. Then she made a comment about how when all the people were gone she'd bet this place didn't feel like 'him'. Which was what I'd thought earlier too, only she'd put it so much better than I could have.

He grinned, sidled closer to her. "Now how do you know what I feel like?"

Joking, relaxed, teasing. With her, Lachie was all the things he hadn't been with me. I'd done this all wrong and blown it. Maybe I'd been too late anyway.

Scarlett turned and looked at me, probably waiting for an introduction. That was all she did, but it sent my pulse racing.

"Scarlett, this is…" Lachie's voice tapered off.

This is … nobody. This is…

"Joel Hitchcock," I said, my mouth suddenly dry.

"Yes, Joel's a bass player," he added. "With Black Paisley."

What a way to make a lousy impression on a girl. Such a letdown. At least Lachie had remembered the name of the band. It was something.

Scarlett turned to him, asked if he needed an interior architect for his house, didn't push the point.

Then she said, "Nick told me how sick your dad is. I'm sorry to hear it, Lachie."

I'd heard his father had cancer. Maybe I should have mentioned something too but it hadn't seemed right when I barely knew the guy.

She touched Lachie's arm—touched a piece of my

heart if I was going to be honest—then apologized for interrupting, as if there'd been anything for her to interrupt. She seemed to know exactly the right thing to say,

"It's okay, really, no problem at all." Lachie said. "But tonight's not for sickness. It's for drinking."

He raised his beer so I clinked my bottle against his and took a sip even though I didn't feel much like drinking any more.

And I watched Lachie leave, my dreams disappearing with him, dissolving before my eyes. Maybe my vision wasn't as great as Martin Luther King's but I had a dream. Everyone was allowed to dream.

Yep, Lachie had gone, leaving me with a sinking feeling.

And with Scarlett.